# The Scorpion Clan

With six terrible words, the Kami Bayushi set his followers in the newly founded Scorpion Clan on a dark and dangerous path. Enemies loomed beyond Rokugan's borders, but they also lurked within them. Bayushi swore to protect the Empire by any means necessary. Where the Code of Bushidō tied the Emperor's Left and Right Hands, the Emperor's Underhand could still reach. To combat the liars, traitors, and thieves within the Great Clans, Bayushi's followers would have to lie, cheat, and steal in turn. The weapons of the Scorpion became blackmail, poison, and sabotage. The Scorpion dirtied their hands so that others' could remain pure.

Each Scorpion family specializes in a different sort of deception, wearing masks as an overt promise of their duplicity. The ruling family of the Scorpion, the Bayushi, are master manipulators and swift swordsmen. The Shosuro, meanwhile, seem but a family of talented artists and actors, but from their ranks come the clan's spies and saboteurs, their poisoners and assassins. The Soshi, a family of *shugenja*, have mastered the subtle art of calling upon the kami silently. Some claim the Soshi wield the shadows themselves as a weapon or a shield. Finally, the Yogo, a family of shugenja cursed to betray the ones they love, protect the Empire from those who delve into forbidden, evil magics.

Yet, in spite of—and perhaps because of—the clan's fearsome reputation, there is none more loyal than a Scorpion. In a clan of deceivers and manipulators, trust is a hard-earned treasure to be cherished and guarded. Betrayal is punished with swift retribution, the souls of the treacherous forever bound into the horrific limbo of the place known as Traitor's Grove. Such fierce loyalty is a small consolation, at least, given the dangerous but vital role the Scorpion have played in the Empire from the moment their Kami spoke his fateful words: "I will be your villain, Hantei."

Cover illustration by Amélie Hutt.

Map illustration by Francesca Baerald.

Color insert artwork by Mauro Dal Bo, Amélie Hutt, Pavel Kolomeyets,
Niten, Chris Ostrowski, Borja Pindado, Polar Engine, and Scott Wade.

ISBN: 978-1-63344-339-6
Printed in China.

Fantasy Flight Games
1995 West County Road B2
Roseville, MN 55113
USA

Find out more about Fantasy Flight Games
and our many exciting worlds at

**www.FantasyFlightGames.com**

A
# Legend of the Five Rings™

*novella*

# Whispers of Shadow and Steel

By Mari Murdock

Fantasy Flight Games

Unicorn Lands

Dragon Lands

Phoenix Lands

Lion Lands

**SOSHI CASTLE**

**CITY OF LIES**

**OTOSAN UCHI**

**YOGO CASTLE**

**SHOSURO CASTLE**

**BAYUSHI PALACE**

Shinomen Forest

Scorpion Lands

Northern Crane Lands

Crab Lands

Southern Crane Lands

The Shadowlands

Islands of Silk and Spice

Rokugan

# Chapter One

Bayushi Yojiro chafed his hands together as his rickshaw crept along Mercantile Avenue in Ryokō Owari Toshi, the City of Lies. The Scorpion Clan rarely grants second chances, and his had come in the form of exile to the most indulgent—and dangerous—city in Rokugan. He shrank behind his high collar. What trap lurked behind the decadence?

The well-worn cobblestones of the famed Merchant Quarter were nearly invisible beneath the crowds of people bursting from shops and milling between tents. The pounding clamor of street musicians' cymbals shook the air, mingling with oppressive clouds of heavy perfume, cooking oil, and sweat. Around the merchants and buyers, teetering mountains of silks, dried tea leaves, exotic fruits, incense, lacquerware, and spices sprawled like the Spine of the World Mountains themselves. Voices clashed in the ruckus of trade, sellers bellowing prices and guaranteeing bargains, customers haggling and comparing quality. A red silk palanquin with a horned roof, belonging perhaps to some noble lady, sliced through the crowd. It disappeared as swiftly as it had come, born aloft by six heavily muscled servants, gliding above the market's commotion like a pleasure barge atop the writhing sea.

Travelers from all the Great Clans mingled in a chaos of hues. A Crane Clan noblewoman, dressed in a flowing blue kimono with a crown of silk flowers atop her white hair, inspected the artistry of some tapestries while her *yōjimbō* kept the crowds at bay. A pair of gruff Unicorn Clan warriors, trimmed in bear-fur boots and armed with sleek Moto scimitars, disputed the price for a cage of rare falcons. A towering Crab samurai with a missing ear elbowed everyone in his path as he followed the beckoning glances of *maiko* geisha in luxurious gowns, who giggled as they headed toward the ferry wharves to sail back to the Licensed Quarter.

Yojiro huddled in his rickshaw, overwhelmed by the swell and clangor of the masses, so different from the immaculate, spacious streets and neatly sorted bazaars of Otosan Uchi. He had left the capital city expecting difference, knowing Ryokō Owari's reputation for being "a gilded ruin," but this grinding disorder was proving oppressive. Perhaps Ryokō Owari Toshi—"Journey's End City"—was far enough away from the Heavenly Sovereign to avoid the Emperor's Celestial influence.

The darkness bothered Yojiro the most. Above his head rattled rows of the city's red-and-black Scorpion Clan banners and clusters of paper lanterns. These, strung between the unnaturally wide eaves of the sloped rooftops, crowded the air above, which seemed as full as the streets. They blocked much of the sunlight and cast long, deep shadows even at midday. The dimness played tricks on his eyes; when he passed a vendor, he thought she was selling human skulls. Only when a woman put one on her face did Yojiro realize they were actually theater masks. Another time, a horned *oni* emerged from a tofu shop, driving his hand to his katana. The demon was a child upon her father's shoulders, her horns two looped braids in her hair. Yojiro could only curse himself for being a fool so many times before he eventually stopped looking.

Yojiro's rickshaw puller, a sun-scorched peasant with a pocked face, eased to a halt, paused, and stared as though waiting for something. The buffeting wall of merchants and tourists among the goods and kiosks was as thick as ever, and he seemed hesitant to aggressively pitch himself into the swarm. He let go of the handrail to wipe sweat from his brow.

"We are almost at Shosuro Palace, Magistrate," he croaked to Yojiro. "Just past this bazaar, through the Pious Gate, beyond the wall, and all the way—"

"Yes, thank you," Yojiro said, cutting off the man's exaggerated account of the route. Shosuro Palace's sloped granite foundation and crimson-tiled keep rose mere streets away, not more than a half hour's stroll. "I think I shall walk from here."

"No, no, no," the man objected, picking up the handrail again but making no effort to press on. "You said to the palace, so I will take you."

"I will still pay you for the rest of the journey," Yojiro assured the puller, ignoring the man's insistent greed. He drew a green silk purse from his pocket, a recess safely sewn deep in the breast of his black-and-crimson kimono. "I did say to the palace, so you will get that fare."

The rickshaw puller grinned stupidly, an air of self-congratulation at his slyness wrinkled into his pitted cheeks. The dim light crinkled the man's face into a more demonic visage than the little girl's. Yojiro ignored the impulse to squint, just to be sure. He tossed the man his coins and barely had time to step down into the street before the puller vanished, adeptly ducking into a dark alley, rickshaw and all.

*This would never happen to an Emerald Magistrate in Otosan Uchi. And this trick from a member of my own clan.*

He folded his hands into his kimono sleeves and stepped into the masses.

*I suppose that in a pit full of scorpions, some begin to eat one another.*

As though instantiating his thoughts, the nimble fingers of a pickpocket suddenly tickled his side. Hand in Yojiro's side pocket, the small boy pretended to stare at a grotesque dancing dog. Yojiro let the tiny hand scuttle away disappointed. The child scampered toward the same alley as the rickshaw puller, and the peasant's pockmarked oni face jutted out from the shadows. He grabbed the boy by the collar, cursing and reaching inside his own kimono to indicate the location of Yojiro's purse. His eyes seethed with fury as he spotted Yojiro watching them from the crowd. The conspirators vanished into the dark alley again, like rats into their hole.

*They aren't the only thieves.*

Yojiro had already noticed dozens of tricksters in the bazaar, cheating customers and each other. Some used scales with false centers of balance or chains of differing metals to weight one side more than another. Others used abacuses with fixed beads or movable bead columns to falsely calculate prices and cargo quantities. And nearly every merchant could deftly palm coins or cut purse strings. Some even tried to hide their affiliation with the Scorpion, masquerading as peddlers from Minor Clans, their exaggerated country dialects and cheap costumes with shoddily embroidered badgers or foxes actually fooling the tourists. Many, just like Yojiro's two rats, emerged from or disappeared into dark alleys flanked with looming walls and occluded by sweeping tile roofs. The dim shade of the narrow passageways concealed their movements, probably by design.

As one would expect from the Scorpion Clan's most visited city.

The Scorpion crest woven across the front of Yojiro's clothes suddenly felt heavy, a burden. Everyone could see it. Anyone might assume he was like those scorpions in the pit. A liar. Always concealing something. They might think this even though he was a samurai, sworn to uphold the sacred tenets of Bushidō, embracing virtues like Righteousness, Sincerity, Honor. Virtues he would gladly give his life to uphold.

*But what about your soul, Yojiro?*

A disturbing memory wriggled in the back of his mind. Bleak trees wreathed with empty armor and broken blades. A frigid wind stirred the leaves, but all else lay still.

He immediately shoved it away.

A Scorpion banner flapped before him in the mild breeze. The crest's tail hung over him, as if about to strike, poised and waiting for the right moment.

*Am I really one of them?*

He wandered past a few more stands when the pickpocket, squat and skulking in the dimness like a goblin, appeared again. The boy casually snipped the strings of a tall Dragon Clan woman's coin pouch as he snuck by. In two strides, Yojiro was at his side, clutching his shoulder in a firm fist. Wordlessly, he snatched the money from the boy's fingers.

"Excuse me," Yojiro called to the woman. He held out her purse. "I am afraid you dropped this by accident."

The woman eyed Yojiro and the boy suspiciously, snatching her bag from him. "Yes, that is mine," she snapped, forcing it open to count her coins. Assured of its contents, she let her face soften. "Daikoku be praised for preserving my money. I shall say an extra prayer at his temple in thanks." She smiled until her eyes fell upon the Scorpion Clan crest on his clothes. She marched away with no second glance. Yojiro bit his lip. Perhaps it had been a poor choice to approach the Dragon, given the circumstances...

Yojiro had been sent to Ryokō Owari to arbitrate a scandal involving the Dragon Clan. Bayushi Aramoro, half brother to the Scorpion Clan Champion, Bayushi Shoju, had been arrested for killing a minor Dragon official. The involvement of such a high-ranking samurai threatened the already strained diplomatic relations between the two clans.

"He stands accused of murder without cause," Akodo Toturi had explained in their private meeting back in Otosan Uchi. The Lion Clan samurai's generally inscrutable demeanor had cracked under the situation's strain; his eyes clouded as his mind reeled through possible resolutions. "Naturally, a minor death like this would result in few repercussions. However, the present moment finds this news most inopportune, coming on the heels of that *iaijutsu* duel between Kitsuki Shomon and Bayushi Gensato to resolve a public insult and amid suspicion that the Dragon petition about the Perfect Land Sect was sabotaged by Scorpion-spread gossip. Yes, the two clans are at each other's throats. I have heard rumors of annulments and even blatant violations of treaties between the two sides."

"It surely is not as bad as you say, Toturi-sama," Yojiro had said.

"Perhaps, but I received a personal visit from Kitsuki Yaruma, Dragon Clan liaison to the Imperial Capital. He hinted at the possibility of trade embargoes against the Scorpion. Such a move would demand other political retaliation. This situation could very well spiral out of control for the Empire."

Yojiro had been confused. In his earlier meetings with Lady Kachiko and other Scorpion nobles about long-term diplomatic strategies, he had heard no whisper of intent to increase political difficulty with the Dragon. He also couldn't believe that Lord

Shoju would let his own half brother be implicated in such a petty ordeal as a minor official's death. Especially on the cusp of a major political battle. Let alone publicly! It simply was not their way. Too blatant. Too sloppy. If Aramoro had been caught and imprisoned, he had let himself be caught and imprisoned.

*But what could our clan gain from such a scandal as the public killing of a minor Dragon official?*

As if the Emerald Champion could read his mind, Toturi had answered, "Yojiro-san, I do not know what advantage the Scorpion hope for in implicating Aramoro in such trouble. However, you and I can guess that they have a plan in place. And you and I can also guess that Governor Shosuro Hyobu and her administrators will likely interfere with the investigations surrounding this incident. I have already addressed some of Yaruma's complaints by arranging for Aramoro to be held somewhere other than the Shosuro Palace dungeons, and I have ordered the city's Emerald Magistrate, Otomo Seno, to take charge of the inquiry. However, I have need of further assurances on the matter."

"What would the Emerald Champion ask of me?"

"I know you have already done me a great favor, Yojiro-san, to the detriment of your reputation among your clan," he said, referring to the Tournament of the Emerald Champion. Yojiro had tilted his head, as if ignorant of what Toturi referred to. As the tournament overseer, Yojiro had covertly warned Toturi of a Scorpion plot to sabotage the duel, helping Toturi win but losing the trust of his clan. To acknowledge such an act publicly would be admitting to acting against his clan. "I did no such favor, my lord," he said, warning Toturi with his eyes.

In turn, Toturi had hesitated, pausing to recant his improper assertion against Yojiro's honor.

"I must have been mistaken. Forgive me." A quick calculation troubled his face before he spoke again. "But I now ask you, for the sake of honor, will you go to Ryokō Owari Toshi as my representative, help in the investigation, and prevent any…interference?"

Toturi's request had pounded a sore spot in Yojiro's heart. His clan already mistrusted him. To challenge them with the Emerald Champion's authority would be political suicide.

His age-old conflict between loyalty to country and loyalty to clan had boiled within him once again, but he had answered the Emerald Champion without hesitation.

"I will do as you ask."

He was sincere in his desire to obey Toturi, to prevent dishonorable acts from impeding the investigation, but he could not afford another damning failure as far as the Scorpion were concerned.

"Uncle, you're hurting my shoulder!" the pickpocket hissed, wriggling in Yojiro's grip. He kicked Yojiro's shins to no effect. "Let me go!" A pit grew in Yojiro's stomach as he observed the child's grimy hair and pouting tears.

*I have cheated this boy twice today.*

Again, his responsibility as a samurai demanded action. Courtesy. Compassion. Yojiro scattered a few coins onto the ground for the urchin before releasing him. The boy scooped up the money and dashed away, disappearing into another rathole. A brazen ointment seller suddenly latched onto Yojiro's arm and shoved a box of pungent slime into his face. The acrid perfume of sulfur and fermenting ginger grated in his nose. "For your wrinkles!" the man cried. "Your troubles age you, sir. But today you are in luck! I discovered this special formula after being blessed by Jurōjin with a dream. A vision of longevity! This paste will dissolve all your sorrows—"

Flames suddenly erupted from a fried-noodle stand, causing nearby cages of monkeys to shriek. Yojiro took the interruption to flee, melting in the crowd.

Soon, he turned down Alabaster Street, hoping to skirt the rest of the bazaar's seething commotion, on his way to Shosuro Palace. The avenue was narrow and infested with openings to tunneling alleys. As he walked briskly, he felt a prickle at the back of his neck. He hesitated. The dark corners were vacant, but out of the corner of his eye, it seemed a blood-red mist was lilting past the far end of the alley to his right. He turned. The alley was vacant: it was just an empty shadow.

Yojiro stopped walking, gripping his katana at the mouth of its scabbard.

"Who is there?" he called.

The skinny pickpocket slinked out of the shadows.

"Uncle, you forgot something," the boy called out, grinning in malicious amusement.

"What is that, child?"

Yojiro smelled the waft of gutter flesh too late. A pair of hands snaked under his arms and coiled up behind his head, pulling his grip from his katana's hilt and rendering his arms immobile in the air. The rank, wheezing breath and greasy skin of his captor identified him as the rickshaw puller. With ease, Yojiro slipped down, out of the man's grip, and slammed an elbow blow deep into his belly. The puller fell, gasping.

Yojiro turned to speak to the boy again, but the child was gone. Instead, the alley was now blocked by the red silk palanquin with the horned roof. Its six lumbering servants set it down and glared at Yojiro with brutish ferocity. From behind the crimson curtain, a sumptuously dressed man emerged. Strings of onyx beads wound about his neck and shoulders, and he had several golden teeth. The Scorpion Clan crest was embroidered across the collar and sleeves of his kimono, but the wicked gleam in his eye proved more revealing. This was evidently one of Ryokō Owari's crime lords.

"The child is right, Magistrate," the man said, his voice calm, reassured: the tone of a man used to getting everything he wanted. He brandished a long, carnelian-and-brass pipe in the shape of a scorpion, its blue-gray smoke seeping between his sneering lips. "You forgot that this is not in your jurisdiction. As a citizen assigned to the neighborhood watch, I am the one obliged to mete out justice here. Isn't that right, Buyu?"

"Yes, Ikku-sama," the rickshaw puller confirmed, a hint of cringing fear in his voice. "This quarter is yours."

"Ha ha. He exaggerates." Ikku laughed. "But, what you did to that poor boy—stealing his money—and just now to this rickshaw puller is inexcusable. In my duty to uphold this neighborhood's peace, I cannot tolerate robbers and brawlers. As a magistrate yourself, surely you must understand this."

Yojiro folded his hands into his sleeves, a feigned gesture of humility as he calculated the speed with which he could draw his sword should words not work. Despite his training, six guards in a narrow backstreet would prove difficult, and he had no idea what other minions Ikku might command forth from the shadows.

"Pardon my intrusion, sir," Yojiro said, ignoring the temptation to eye the other dark corners of the street. He needed confidence now. Composure. Delicacy. "I am unfamiliar with your local rules, having only just arrived in Ryokō Owari from the capital on official business for the Emerald Champion."

The crime lord smiled, his teeth glimmering in the dimness. He rudely pointed at Yojiro with his pipe. "Surely, coming from Otosan Uchi, you should know that not even Emerald Magistrates are above the law."

"No, we are not," Yojiro agreed. "Then, I humbly ask forgiveness. I shall refrain from further troubling you and these humble people."

"Forgiveness is insufficient for justice's demands, Magistrate," the crime lord chortled. He spilled the spent ashes in his pipe into the street and signaled his enforcers toward Yojiro with a casual gesture.

Yojiro lowered his stance slightly, centering his balance to react to an attack. "Perhaps I might ask Governor Hyobu to help me satisfy the demands of your justice. Doesn't her Thunder Guard enforce the governor's law here?"

"They could if they were here, but you are lucky I got to you first, Magistrate. They are less…understanding than I am. The Kami only know how many cells these Thunder Guard fill. How many bodies they leave behind. Since you have only slightly wronged these gentle citizens, I ask you pay a small fine to clear up this misunderstanding. Then you can avoid a more…enthusiastic punishment."

"His purse is in a breast pocket!" Buyu called out.

The crime lord nodded. His brutes were now within striking range. "Now, Magistrate, you have a simple choice. Pay the fine and continue on your important 'official' business. Or…"

Yojiro grimaced. Duty demanded his mission take priority. Even if he could win this battle, angering a local crime lord might make his task more difficult, especially if he were to get caught up on the wrong side of the Thunder Guard. For now, he had to bend with the wind.

He drew his green purse and threw it. Ikku caught it, rubbing the coins inside, smirking.

"This is the right choice, Magistrate," he said, climbing back into his palanquin. "Enjoy your stay in our city. I look forward to seeing you again."

The gang members dispersed, each disappearing into a different rathole, leaving Yojiro alone. Hopefully. He double-checked the shadows to see if the alleys were empty. Nothing moved, yet the exaggerated eaves of the surrounding buildings made the dark unfathomable from a few paces away.

*Curse the architect.*

Yojiro finally left Alabaster Street, the road ending in front of a twenty-foot stone wall, the perimeter separating the Merchant Quarter from the Noble Quarter. He approached the Pious Gate, an enormous entrance with lintels studded in gold flowers and carved with peacocks, tigers, and scorpions. Its imposing bronze-bound doors cast the illusion of an oasis in the midst of the bazaar's turmoil, promising refinement and order beyond its threshold. But Yojiro knew better.

*If the Merchant Quarter is this city's den of thieves, then surely I will find Ryokō Owari's master deceivers in the Noble Quarter. If I am not careful, I may lose more than my purse.*

# Chapter Two

*Y*ojiro squinted in the faint light, the bare walls and exceptionally thick *shōji* paper of the window screens offering no sense of direction in the mazelike halls of Shosuro Palace. He only kept his bearings by noticing subtle blemishes in the cherry floorboards, but the dimness made those difficult to follow.

*Even the palace is a dark alley.*

He was escorted by a squad of four spear-wielding Thunder Guard soldiers and their captain, Shosuro Denmaru. Their red-and-black armor mingled with the shadows, and the crimson plumes atop their helmets trailed after them like bloody streams.

*Did Ikku speak the truth about them?*

Denmaru's wrinkles and a patch of fire-scarred flesh on the left side of his jaw gave his face the illusion of being carved from rough stone. A slight limp indicated an old injury on the same side, but the samurai's adjusted gait did nothing to hinder his balance or precision of footfall. His hands also bore scorch marks.

"How long have you been in the service of Governor Hyobu, Captain?" Yojiro asked.

"Her whole career," he answered, his gaze fixed on their path through the labyrinth. "I was her yōjimbō before being assigned to the Thunder Guard when she became governor."

"She must put a great deal of faith in you to have kept you so close for over twenty years," Yojiro replied, hoping his compliment would soften the Shosuro samurai.

"Hyobu-sama does whatever is necessary." Denmaru grunted absently. "As do I."

"Naturally. I have heard great stories about the Thunder Guard," Yojiro continued. "Its long history boasts many impressive feats. Defending the city from Lion Clan invasions centuries ago. Battling the opium cartels. Breaking up smuggling rings. Saving the Noble Quarter from fires."

Denmaru did not flinch at the word "fire" as Yojiro had anticipated. Instead, the captain smiled with puckered lips, as if the word conjured a bittersweet memory. "The work of my comrades to control this city is indeed valiant."

"Surely, yours as well. It seems we in Otosan Uchi heard news of the last fire only…six or seven years ago."

The captain merely shrugged. "I helped."

Yojiro huddled back into his high collar. Toturi's request for him to prevent Scorpion interference specifically referred to working around Hyobu and her Thunder Guard, and this aloof conversation proved worrisome.

Will she be as difficult to work with?

Finally, the appearance of a lavish silk and cloth-of-gold curtain broke the uniformity of the hallways. Denmaru parted the brocade silently with a strong arm, revealing another dark room.

"Governor Hyobu is in here."

"Thank you, Captain," Yojiro replied. "You have been an immense help."

The Thunder Guard and his infantry merely marched away, the darkness of the corridor swallowing them.

Yojiro entered the parlor, but the maze of gossamer canopies and tapestried hangings tangled in a pall of fragrant brazier smoke proved blinding. His eyes slowly attuned to the gloom, revealing the room's furnishings. Between the tangle of silk and drapery, decorative screens and curtains of ivory beads concealed all walls, masking the true size of the room. Every few paces revealed rearing dark brass statues of frolicking animals. Or dancers? Rare ebony porcelain vases balanced on every flat surface, filled with glinting paper poppies that seemed to shudder in the flickering candlelight in dizzying movements. Despite having only just entered, Yojiro felt that even the direction of the door might disappear if he were not careful.

"Excuse me, Governor Hyobu-sama," he called, blinking as he crept farther into the room. "I am Bayushi Yojiro, the Emerald Magistrate newly arrived from Otosan Uchi."

Silence greeted his salutation. To be sure he was alone, Yojiro squinted again. None of the dim shapes moved.

He nearly stumbled upon a heap of silk cushions that blended seamlessly into a sumptuous rug, both half-hidden in the dimness. Beyond the strewn cushions stood scarlet-lacquered furniture arranged around a circular table. He drew close to examine its craftsmanship. An antique set, from the last century. Red cedarwood, probably sourced from the nearby Kinbō Province. Beautiful, though the lacquerwork was slightly flawed. He drew a curious finger along the minutely uneven paint layers on the back of a chair. But it was smooth, well cared for. The seats and divan had even been reupholstered with new silk, gold and pale jade threads marking them current with the present fashion season.

Yojiro moved to sit but froze as a tiny gleam of light caught his attention, like the twinkle in the eyes of a cat. He peered into the shadows. Nothing. The light had vanished. Or had he really seen it at all?

The points of his high, arching collar pricked the sides of his face, as if to spur his discomfort. He pulled at them, freeing his chin.

"My, you are as handsome as they say, aren't you?" The sudden, crooning voice split through the silence.

Yojiro blinked, his heart and breath tightening inside his ribs as he wildly scanned the parlor once more. Only the dark, lonely furnishings populated the room. A sheen of sweat prickled across his body.

*She is toying with you. She is a Shosuro, after all, and they like their secret nets.*

"Hyobu-sama," he began again, bowing formally to the dark. He reached into his sleeve to withdraw his papers of introduction. "My name is—"

"I heard you the first time, Yojiro-san," the unseen woman

trilled, amusement curling her vowels as she uttered his name. "And no need for your papers. I have my own information."

A hand appeared, as if floating, above the carpet, and slowly, the gentle curves of one of the brass statues sharpened into a stunning woman, graceful and sensuous in her middle age, swathed in layers of gold and crimson kimono despite the glowering heat of the braziers. She wore a black silk tulle veil over the lower half of her face instead of a mask. Her eyes, though slightly wilted by time, stared sharp and sparkling through the dimness. She had been administering to one of the vases, shaping its counterfeit bouquet with a tiny pair of shears. She beckoned Yojiro closer with a gold-lacquered fingernail. The heavy, spiced smells of poppy milk and plum wine wafted around her.

"It is a pleasure to meet you, Hyobu-sama," he said, bowing again, this time in her actual direction. "I hope I do not intrude on your busy schedule. Denmaru was kind enough to show me in."

Hyobu's lips curled behind her gossamer veil. "He is a dutiful servant. We were expecting you, of course."

"Then perhaps you know why I have come to Ryokō Owari."

"Yes," Hyobu replied, grasping his hands in an overly cordial manner, her skin hot against his. Yojiro had no idea where her snipping shears had gone. "I heard that you have come to my lovely city on urgent business, but you must make time to explore our Licensed Quarter. We have such pleasures to be enjoyed there. The finest wines. Gardens of the rarest flowers. Dramatic and glorious theater. The most meticulously trained *onna* geisha and *otoko geisha*. Everything to soothe or charm your senses."

"Another time, perhaps."

"Too bad. I heard the Cherry Petal Grove has just acquired a talented flautist."

Yojiro shook his head, politely. Hyobu shrugged and guided him to a seat. She then waved her hand, and immediately the mound of cushions stood. Yojiro's breath caught in his throat. The silken pillows had merely been a servant girl, kneeling prostrate upon the floor. She skipped across the room to retrieve a lacquered tea set. Returning, she poured him a generous cup of emerald-colored tea before retreating back to her post, again merging into the decor.

He cast his eyes around the room again for more surprises.

"I have heard interesting stories about you, Yojiro-san," the governor crooned, clicking her fingernails against the teacup. "I hear you are a masterful artisan. Carpentry, is it?"

"Carving, primarily, but it is only a hobby," he replied. "I have had no formal training."

"But I heard that you are talented beyond the need for a sensei. Last year, everyone spoke of a mahogany *inrō* box you made for your sister to hang from her obi that made every woman in the capital jealous."

"Surely, that was only due to Mikuru's kind praise of my work," he mumbled, the mention of his sister pricking his heart. Had Hyobu heard of their dissociation? "Do you mind if we speak about why I came? I do not wish to trespass upon your time."

"Well, since you are so adamant about business, instead of pleasure, I suppose we should get on with it," Hyobu said, delicately sipping her tea beneath her gossamer veil. "I am glad you have been sent to clear up this scandal surrounding Aramoro. It truly is unfortunate that he was caught up in the death of Kitsuki Obo."

"Then you already believe him to be innocent?" Yojiro asked, his tongue tickling from the strange tea blend.

"Don't you, Yojiro-san?"

Yojiro frowned. "I was sent by Champion Toturi to discover the truth."

Hyobu smiled coyly, her bright eyes narrowing. "Of course. The truth."

"Do you have any information concerning the circumstances of Kitsuki-sama's death that might aid me?"

"Not really." She laughed. "I generally leave matters of murder in Denmaru's hands."

Yojiro stiffened, the insinuation seeming too blatant.

"Oh?" Yojiro continued, shielding the newly broached skepticism from his voice and replacing it with interest. "He is investigating this case, then."

"He did at first. When the body was first discovered in the Fishers' Quarter. However, Champion Toturi has since commanded the case be left to the Emerald Magistrates. To calm the cries of Dragon hatchlings, I suppose. You see, I have been receiving heated letters from Dragon Clan and Kitsuki family representatives all week. Pages and pages of complaints and bile. Though I am tired of their bawling, their letters have indicated several serious economic ramifications for my city."

"Such as?"

"Bans on Dragon trade ships entering our Bay of Drowned Honor. Normally, I would not balk at such threats. The Dragon have very few exports that I care about. Crystals. Monastery books. The occasional alchemical ingredients. You know, curios that only those with very specific tastes would enjoy. However, this threat may also bar us from their gold market, which, I'm afraid to admit, would be a severe blow. That market keeps us competitive with the other trade centers throughout Rokugan, and without it, my economy might just shrivel up."

She paused to sip more tea. She was pretending not to study Yojiro's eyes.

"Excuse my rambling concerns. They are nothing more than the fears of a pressed administrator. I am also aware of your concerns in this matter, Yojiro-san, since this case involves certain personal investments for you, too. Lady Kachiko has informed me extensively regarding what those might be," Governor Hyobu warbled nonchalantly.

A tiny spasm in Yojiro's chest threatened to unravel into despair at the mention of Bayushi Kachiko. That dark, bleeding memory rippled again.

The Tournament of the Emerald Champion. The Lion Clan winning over the Scorpion. He winced, remembering how his clan had rejected him. "Failure," they had whispered. "Traitor." Even his own dear sister Mikuru. At his request, she had been ready to risk her own life for the part she played to secure a Scorpion victory. When his plan failed, rendering her sacrifice for naught, she refused to speak to him ever again. But beyond becoming a social outcast, the pain—that searing shame—came from the look Kachiko had given him. Her dark eyes. Deep and alive, like fiery pools of pitch. She had even taken off her mask to stare, intense and hateful, into his own face. She had looked so beautiful, even in her fury, the grace of her cheek only enriched by her ire.

"Your failure was unfortunate, Yojiro," she had said, her usually refined, alluring diplomacy poisoned in her disgust. "You play at maintaining your integrity, but where is the honor when a master has an unreliable servant? Your failure betrayed my trust, Yojiro. You betrayed me."

Had he truly betrayed her? His resolve to serve Rokugan, to serve the Empire over the Scorpion, might have held. He had, after all, devotedly accomplished his duty to the Emperor as his Emerald Magistrate. He had righted a wrong under Heaven. He had restored balance, harmony, justice. He had upheld his oaths to follow Bushidō...

Yet Kachiko's dark eyes still haunted him. Her look pierced his heart with a hundred hot needles. Beyond the fire of her wrath glimmered a shard of hurt. A wound, bruised and bleeding. He had inflicted it. His failure had inflicted it.

He had betrayed Kachiko. For that, he could not forgive himself.

And she had reminded him that the Scorpion Clan could not forgive it, either. She had dismissed him, then held him back for a final message.

"Do not fail me again, Yojiro. To fail twice might mark you a traitor. Traitor's Grove is such a cold place. I would hate to have to visit you there."

In her indifferent mention of Kachiko, Governor Hyobu had been reminding him what was really at stake here in Ryokō Owari. Should he fail, Scorpion *shugenja* would bind his soul to a tree in Traitor's Grove. His final resting place would be in the forest hung with the belongings of other Scorpion traitors, a living tomb wherein he could be tormented for all eternity, unable to advance to the afterlife. A bleak reminder to future generations of Scorpion of the cost for betraying their clan.

Yojiro wrenched the memory away from his eyes.

*This is like the Unicorn Clan parable about the hare caught between the serpent and the hawk, isn't it? Either choice means death... To fail the Scorpion would mean having my soul stolen from me. But to free Aramoro might mean abandoning my oaths to uphold Bushidō, blaspheming under Heaven and losing my soul. Why must my clan duty ever be at odds with my duty to Rokugan?*

"The Mother of Scorpions wishes you luck in your endeavors here," Governor Hyobu continued, clipping the final tangles of his reverie, taunting him.

Yojiro blushed but did not look away, meeting her challenge with a clenched jaw. "Then I carry her blessing with me. And as an Emerald Magistrate, representative of our Emerald Champion and our joint master the Emperor, Son of Heaven, I carry Celestial blessings as well."

Hyobu laughed, her clever eyes narrowing into crescents of delight. "I can see why Lady Kachiko adores you. You are so amusing. Well, if you will protect my city by clearing up this Kitsuki business, I do not see why I should not also add my blessing to theirs. You have my aid. Denmaru is at your service."

"I thank you humbly, Hyobu-sama. However, I could not intrude upon your generosity," he replied, remembering his promise to Toturi. He switched into the furtive language of the court. Delicacy and tact. "I am sure that you and your retainers have much more pressing tasks in this blossoming city than to assist me in such a lowly inquest. I would hate for you and your agents to trouble yourselves."

Hyobu's brows furrowed, though her smile never left her face. "I see. I thank you for your humble thoughtfulness, but as this is my city, I should make a poor governor if I neglected the small tasks. And I would make a poor hostess if I were to simply abandon you in your work."

"Not at all, Hyobu-sama. Instead, you have been a most generous hostess, and from what I have seen of your city, an exceptionally adept leader. No, you would do me great honor if you would trust me with this humble assignment. It would allow me to redeem myself in the eyes of my peers," Yojiro insisted.

Hyobu sniffed, unable to further deny his requests without insulting him. "Your skills garner my confidence, Yojiro-san. At least allow me to assign Denmaru to you as a guide to the city and its workings."

"I am sure that the city's Emerald Magistrate and his *yoriki* are more than capable of helping me."

"Ah yes, Otomo Seno-sama and his investigators." Hyobu chuckled, her dry, delighted sarcasm calming her frustration at his outmaneuvering. "He is quite the warrior for truth and justice here in Ryokō Owari. Always thinking. Always planning. You can take your letters of introduction to the manor of the Emerald

Magistrate to find him. I hear he has made such…interesting improvements to the place."

"Thank you, Hyobu-sama." Yojiro stood, bowing to her politely, though not cordially. He turned to find the door.

"Oh, and Yojiro-san, you may want to visit our Temple Quarter and make an offering at the Temple of Daikoku," Hyobu added, standing and plopping an empty green silk purse onto the table. It was his. "I heard from Denmaru that you…accidentally dropped this. Do be more careful."

# Chapter Three

As Yojiro passed out of the shadow of Shosuro Palace on his way to the Emerald Magistrate's estate, he walked by the magnificent mansions and lush gardens of the Noble Quarter, wary of the odd mirage that seemed to hang in the air. Unlike the Merchant Quarter, this district lay quiet, its few pedestrians silent, not even conferring with one another. A few local dignitaries nodded to him as they passed, only the careful click of their steps echoing after him. Every door and window was shut, all trees and shrubs trimmed to perfection, every cobblestone level and swept. It was all too clean, artificial, like the immaculate skin of a mask.

Yojiro turned a corner, nearly colliding with a man dressed all in black. He leaped back to avoid a crash, his heart pounding. He blinked. The street was empty.

The congested skyline of stunning towers and decorative roofs with pitched eaves crumpled the light of a sinking sun, casting jagged, toothlike shadows on the cobblestones. Many of them, out of the corner of his eye, looked like the faded outline of a person's silhouette. One would never know if one was being followed.

*This district trades dark alleys for illusions. I can't even trust my own shadow here.*

He paused, mid-shudder.

*Could Denmaru or his squad be following me now?*

Yojiro rubbed his eyes. Each shadow still loomed, a possible threat, though he still couldn't see a person casting one. He squeezed a fist around his katana.

*Just be ready for anything. If I keep worrying, these tricks of the light will be the end of me.*

Even if the Thunder Guard was following him, he had nothing to hide from them. He and Hyobu had the same goal. She had obviously received a letter from Kachiko informing her of Yojiro's potential fate in Traitor's Grove, which meant she knew his interests hinged on a favorable Scorpion Clan outcome. Her aims were similar, the potential political threat to her city necessitating a diplomatic triumph over the Dragon by clearing up the scandal. And she had insisted that Yojiro accept her help.

Yet, her words seemed too obvious. "I generally leave matters of murder in Denmaru's hands." Why take such a risk? Was she merely testing his loyalty? Was the Thunder Guard somehow involved, or had she simply referred to their role as her law enforcers? If Ikku's words were to be trusted in any way, the Thunder Guard had a reputation for merciless, perhaps even corrupt, practices. Could that be under Hyobu's command? Was Ikku one of her minions? Yojiro's purse had certainly made its swift way to her. Or had Denmaru really retrieved Yojiro's purse from the crime lord? According to Ikku's side of the story, they certainly seemed at odds. Regardless, he must be wary of the whole lot of them for now.

*What is Kachiko hoping I do in the face of all these Scorpion secrets?*

Yojiro finally reached the manor of the Emerald Magistrate.

The massive three-story building wrapped around a hollow courtyard open to the street. Unlike other civic centers, which feature traditional Rokugani architecture, this building had no angular roof, no windows, and no shōji screen doors or sliding exterior walls. Instead, the structure was a solid square encasement of pine, like an enormous wooden chest. In contrast to the ugly, ascetic building design, the center of a courtyard featured a large garden waterfall cascading over obelisks made from stacks of square stone blocks. The water flowed into a pool ringed in black marble that bore the inscription "Ritsuryō," the word for Rokugani traditional law.

Near this waterfall, on a stone dais, knelt a rail-thin man swaddled in a pale-green kimono. The Otomo family crest of four coiled snakes was emblazoned across the chest, marking him as a member of one of the Imperial families, those related to the Emperor or counted among his closest followers. However, this Otomo crest was inside an emerald orb, the official marking of an Emerald Magistrate. A black, polished *kanmuri* hat sat pinned upon his grey head, and dark facial hair framed his stern mouth, granting him a regal yet sinister look. He perched behind a tiny bamboo desk scattered with stacks of official papers and scrolls, which he busily perused, occasionally making notes with the flick of a brush. A single man inside an enormous wooden fortress.

Yojiro approached, handing his letter of introduction to a nearby attendant.

"Otomo Seno-sama, I presume." Yojiro bowed low before his fellow magistrate. "I am Bayushi Yojiro, the Emerald Magistrate from Otosan Uchi. I was sent here by the Emerald Champion to aid you in your ongoing investigation of Kitsuki Obo's death."

Seno briefly looked up from his papers, setting down his brush on a plain, square inkstone. His bleak eyes scanned Yojiro before he took the letter of introduction and read it. His mouth puckered. Somewhat loud over the sound of the waterfall, his voice was cold, with a restrained, polite malice.

"You must speak up if I am to hear you, Bayushi-sama." He waved his hand in the direction of the splashing water. "The spies of your clan necessitate this trick."

Yojiro blinked, the Otomo's blunt insinuation rendering him momentarily speechless. "Pardon me?"

"Scorpion spies," Seno said simply, taking up his brush again, finishing some notes in the margin of a scroll. "This city is swarming with them: there is an eavesdropper in every corner. Their presence has required that many measures be taken to maintain peace of mind and peace of city, and this waterfall ensures my privacy in the execution of my duties." With this, he once more eyed Yojiro warily, subtly leaning away as if afraid of being stung.

Yojiro paused, a protest forming on his lips, but he maintained his courtly respect and composure. He smiled before answering. "I understand that the exaggerated reputation of my clan might alarm you into a state of perpetual concern, Seno-sama. However, you must forgive my skepticism. I have never known such precautions to seem necessary, let alone be taken, even in Otosan Uchi."

"Are you suggesting that I am paranoid, Bayushi-sama?" Seno frowned, his bony chest puffing up in egotistic agitation as he flung down Yojiro's introduction letter. "Having been Emerald Magistrate in this city for nearly three decades, I have witnessed plenty of proof of your clan's 'reputation.' Especially here, where the agents of the Scorpion seem to cling to our very shadows! Dozens of spies, lurking. Behind every corner. Inside every crack. Watching. Listening. Biding their time…"

A stone formed between Yojiro's ribs, sinking slowly into his belly. He silently groaned.

*Did I sound just as absurd when I told myself these same things about the Thunder Guard moments ago? Fear makes fools of us, does it not? I must learn to bridle my worry.*

"…The construction of this waterfall was my idea, Bayushi-sama, and since its implementation, we have had no disclosures of internal information circulated. Not a single drop of water escapes this bottle! And this is but one of many ingenious initiatives, numerous in every sector. For example, just look what I have done to the manor. Not a hiding place in it. You see, my policies maintain the peace. I am truly the greatest force in the progressive fight against ninja scum that Rokugan has ever seen."

At this, Yojiro nearly could not contain a burst of laughter. "Please excuse my ignorance, but did you say 'ninja'?" He hid his mouth in his high collar. His mirth at the ridiculous notion and the accompanying pomposity of the magistrate nearly rendered him rude. "Otomo-sama, forgive me, but everyone knows that ninja are not real—merely an oft-told tale circulated by gossipmongers and by storytellers looking for listeners' gold."

Yojiro immediately regretted this statement of fact as Seno's face lightened to a shade of enraged grey.

"This is exactly what I expect from a Scorpion," the magistrate growled, barely restraining himself from pointing at Yojiro. "I know your kind, Bayushi-sama. Nothing but deceptions and excuses, ruses and feints. And you come here believing I am fool enough to accept your tricks just because you have a mandate from the Emerald Champion, but I will not. I am prepared for what you might do here to hide the truth, to save face, to protect your clan's ninja conspiracy—"

Seno's insult was cut short by the swift approach of a contingent of *dōshin* wearing leather caps, who dragged several ragged criminals in chains behind them. The guards were led by a samurai wearing slate-colored *hakama* trousers and a sage kimono bearing the crest of the Seppun, another Imperial family. She briefly laid her light-brown eyes on Yojiro before addressing Seno with a deep, formal bow.

"Otomo-sama. We have arrested the leaders of the Storm Tigers in our raid on the wharf near Moment's Edge Bridge, just as you commanded. We managed to capture all of them at a sake house."

Seno's face lit up in bitter pleasure at the news. "Bayushi-sama, this is my yoriki Seppun Motome-san, a servant who enacts my orders."

The woman flinched ever so slightly at Seno's subordination of her, reducing her status as an Imperial law enforcer for his administration to a mere act of servitude. The old Otomo noticed nothing, grinning and pointing at the prisoners.

"And it seems she has brought proof of the effectiveness of my methods." Seno nearly jeered as he took Motome's report, eyeing Yojiro with glee. "I am proud to show this to you, Bayushi-sama. These villains belong to an elite gang of ninja operating on the outskirts of the Fishers' Quarter. With this capture, I am one step closer to destroying the ninja activity in Ryokō Owari."

Yojiro swallowed the rest of his humor, though it threatened to burst from within him. The "ninja gang" stunk of rotting rice and fish guts and were obviously drunk, nearly reeling over themselves. Dressed in threadbare kimono with the Scorpion Clan insignia clumsily stitched all over them, these ragtag criminals were clearly mere ruffians. They probably hustled the occasional laborer in the poorest parts of town, but crime lords they were not, let alone fabled ninja.

Among the group, Yojiro spotted Buyu, the rickshaw puller. *Ninja indeed.*

Though Seno continued to grin stupidly, bragging about his conquest, the look on Motome's face suggested reticence to join Seno in his expression of triumph at the arrest. The Seppun yoriki had her mouth clamped into a tight line of silent seething, an expression that looked long practiced, probably from years of compounded, unvoiced disagreements with Seno's exaggerations. A slight flush in her cheeks hinted at her embarrassment at Seno's assertion that these reprobates were ninja. A flicker in her eye marked distrust, though of Seno or himself, Yojiro was not yet sure.

"Guards, take the criminals to Ryokō Owari Prison. You can press them for their confessions after they have sobered up," Seno ordered, self-adulation plastered on his withered face. He turned to Motome and handed her Yojiro's introduction letter. "Motome-san, you are ordered by Akodo Toturi-sama, our illustrious Emerald Champion, to include this Scorpion representative in your investigation of the death of Kitsuki Obo. However, despite Toturi-sama's confidence in Bayushi-sama, I do not trust as easily. I personally charge you with watching him carefully, and I will hold you responsible for all his actions. Make sure he does not intervene. And that he does not trick you."

With a nod, he dismissed the both of them and continued to work on his stack of papers.

Yojiro swallowed, hesitant to walk away from the Otomo Emerald Magistrate just yet. He had casually, effortlessly insulted a fellow magistrate and a Great Clan in public. What kind of tactless, ill-bred official was this Otomo?

*Perhaps all his yelling over this ridiculous waterfall has made him a brave fox among the chickens. But brave foxes eventually catch arrows.*

"If you would accompany me, Yojiro-sama," Motome said, tucking Toturi's letter into her sleeve for later perusal. "We can confer in my office at Ji-u Reformatory."

Yojiro shot a final annoyed glance at Seno before following Motome onto the street, heading north, back toward the Merchant Quarter through a different gate. He studied her as they walked. The yoriki stood nearly two heads shorter than himself, yet the severity of her light eyes and scowl lent her an intimidating presence. She never opened her mouth unnecessarily. Probably due to her crooked teeth. She kept her short hair tightly secured in a bun at the base of her skull. Though her katana hilt was woven with pristine silk cords, unworn from lack of use, the strong muscles in her hands indicated that she was still trained in some form of martial skill. Perhaps in the *jitte*—one was tucked into her obi—though the two-pronged sword breaker was often carried more as a symbol of a yoriki's authority than for actual fighting.

"I have heard of you, you know," Motome said, interrupting his scrutiny. Her voice was taut with civility and caution. "I heard you are called 'the only honest Scorpion.'"

"An interesting epithet, is it not?" Yojiro replied. "Given to me by the courtiers in Otosan Uchi. It has definitely proved helpful in my career at court."

Motome frowned. "Then it is not true?" She was indeed careful, picking apart his responses for possible motives and meanings.

"You do not believe my reputation?"

"I do not believe many things," she replied, tucking her arms behind her back. "I have lived long enough among the Imperial families and their political façades, and my duties as yoriki bring me in close contact with the full gamut of swindlers, perjurers, and gossipmongers. For me, actions indicate more truth than a tactful excuse or a well-spun story. Or the gossip of reputation."

Her candidness surprised him. He laughed. "Then I suppose, Motome-san, that as a rule, you do not trust people like me."

"No, I do not." She hesitated, turning to look him in the eye. Despite the chill of her expression, the color of her eyes was warm, almost golden. "But I want to. Especially if we are to work together to discover the mysteries behind this murder. It is just that my experiences in this city with…" She paused as though to avoid saying "Scorpion." "…people will not allow for it."

"I understand. Thank you for your candor, Motome-san. If you truly want to trust me, remember that reputations often stem from actions, not merely gossip. I hope that mine will earn your confidence before we part ways."

Motome smiled. "I hope that too."

"Speaking of liars and storytellers, I noticed your doubt at Otomo-sama's insistence that those Storm Tigers are ninja. That is a foolish tale, to be sure," he said, remembering Buyu for his incompetence and unsubtlety in the Merchant Quarter. "And it seems as though you do not trust Otomo-sama with regard to much more than that."

"What? Oh…no…He is my superior," she stammered, picking

her way through the honorable reply. "There are no contradictions between his beliefs and mine. We really do have a problem here in Ryokō Owari…"

"With ninja?" Yojiro said skeptically.

"With *shinobi*."

The word landed like a blow to Yojiro's gut, paralyzing his whole body. Shinobi? Ninja had been an interesting bit of fictional flair. However, the word "shinobi" evoked the most illegal, even unthinkable, of criminal activities. These legendary master saboteurs and assassins were only spoken of in whispers, and Yojiro had never even heard them mentioned out loud by anyone outside his own clan.

"That is impossible, Motome-san," Yojiro said, his voice deepening to a harsh whisper at her confession. The anxious chill of an irrational fear shuddered down his spine. "The existence of shinobi would imply that the Great Clans are making pernicious affronts to Bushidō, abandoning their honor. Such activities would be in direct conflict with ancient Imperial edicts. No clan would dare stoop to such immorality."

Motome clenched her firsts, as if readying for a physical attack. "Regardless of what might be true in normal society, in the safety of Otosan Uchi, as a yoriki in Ryokō Owari, I have seen enough to warrant my assertion. I intend to help Otomo-sama uncover their secrets," she declared, her brow furrowed. "And I intend to prove they exist."

Yojiro stared at the investigator, bewildered by her revelation. Her forthrightness unnerved him, but he did not know why.

*Could she possibly have ulterior motives in blatantly making such a ridiculous claim? If she were a Scorpion, I could anticipate such a bold move being used to draw some secret from me, to put me on the defensive—to frighten me, even. Like Hyobu. But she is a Seppun. She seems so harmless. Still, there is nothing harmless about mentioning shinobi.*

The pair walked in silence through the Gate of Condescension, reentering the Merchant Quarter with its dark alleys. The budding Hour of the Rooster had called forth promoters of the Licensed Quarter, who mixed among the throngs of people, ringing bells and clacking wooden dowels together, shouting promises of wine, gambling, and plays for the night's entertainment. The setting sun made the already-dark roads even gloomier, so traders and vendors lit the hanging street lanterns, casting an abundance of new shadows across the crowded streets. Gangs of firefighters appeared to monitor their blocks, eyeing the lanterns and the people with disdain, sacks of sand or barrels of water at their feet. The emergence of these bullying neighborhood watchers seemed to warrant extra caution, as the Thunder Guard started to make their rounds, and many samurai and nobles now traveled with their yōjimbō.

However, though everyone towered above her, Motome strolled without hesitation through the throngs. Her reputation, whatever that might be, seemed to keep her quite safe. As she walked by, several merchants vanished into alleys at the sight of her, casting rueful looks in her direction. She merely ambled along, paying them no heed, her arms folded behind her back, her jitte poking out of her obi farther than before, somewhat ominously.

"You are obviously very adept at your work, Motome-san," Yojiro said finally after they turned down Jade Street, finding themselves alone on the quieter lane. "You command the respect of everyone in this quarter."

"It is not me but my station they respect," Motome explained quickly, modestly blushing at the compliment as if unused to any form of recognition.

"Possibly," Yojiro replied. He kept his voice down. "If I may be as honest as you have been with me, I will admit that your previous…declaration came as quite the shock."

She cocked her head, listening intently, though keeping a watchful eye on the alleys.

"Shinobi have not been reality for centuries," Yojiro continued. "So long, in fact, that they are a matter that many now consider only myth."

Motome continued to stroll ahead, her attention mostly on their surroundings, ignoring his explanations. Propriety never left her voice. "You know, Yojiro-sama, I am no liar. What I say always contains all the truth I know. I hope you will give me the benefit of your respect in this matter before we begin our task."

Preventing a grimace from creeping onto his face, Yojiro nodded, opting to defer to her as leader of their investigation and keep further doubts to himself. He would play along for now.

"In fact, we shall start at that point," Motome stated, pulling out a scroll from her obi. It contained an inquiry painting of the face of a man with a small mouth and wispy facial hair. The brushstrokes were fairly well composed—done by someone with training, probably from a Crane art academy—so Yojiro trusted the spite he could see in the portrait's eyes.

"This is Kitsuki Obo, the man whose murder you have come here to help me resolve. He was found in the Fishers' Quarter over two weeks ago, stabbed to death in a sewer gutter."

"Who was he?"

"Kitsuki-sama had been acting as a gold-trade minister for the last twelve years, representing Dragon interests with customers in the Merchant and Fishers' Quarters. However, this was merely a façade."

"Oh?" Yojiro frowned at the detachment with which Motome said this. She was rather calm for someone investigating the secret life of a dead man.

"Yes. He had been acting as my personal informant for about ten of those twelve years, specifically notifying me of shinobi activity in the city."

Yojiro dared another ill-timed laugh. "And you trusted him? Why?"

"Kitsuki-sama was a trained investigator."

Yojiro could not believe his ears. This was the third preposterous thing he had heard in the last hour. The Kitsuki family of the Dragon Clan oversaw an elite magisterial investigation school whose famed ability to scrutinize a scene and deduce the truth from even the tiniest detail rivaled even that of shugenja. For Motome to command such an ally would have been invaluable. His loss would have been equally devastating. Their ten years of correspondence could have made her privy to some of this city's deepest of secrets. Now, Hyobu's insistence on Denmaru's involvement made sense. Motome could be at the heart of something that not just Hyobu but the entire Scorpion Clan would want to keep hidden.

Yojiro now understood why he had been commanded to come here. The murder of a Kitsuki investigator in Ryokō Owari meant that this investigation was dangerous to the Scorpion, given the charge against Aramoro. It made Motome their worst enemy. Against his better judgment, his instinct toward duty, honor, and truth, Yojiro's mind had already begun a defensive analysis of her, constructing ways to conceal his intentions and actions from his new partner, examining her weaknesses and potential points of exploitation.

Torn between the halves of his eternal paradox, Yojiro stared into the painted eyes of Kitsuki Obo's portrait. Their inky blackness nearly professed the sinister plot beginning to emerge.

*To contain this scandal, to save my clan, I may need to stay several steps ahead of Motome. I will need to discover the truth behind this murder before she does. Shinobi or not.*

# Chapter Four

Moments before sunset, the pair arrived at the Ji-u Reformatory on the western bank of the Merchant Quarter near the Bridge of Drunken Lovers. The small compound had thick, towering white-pine walls and an iron gate stained dark with age, a solemn fortress amid the lively markets. The tiny stronghold, built by farmers several centuries before Ryokō Owari was established, had once contained a rice vault for storing reserves for use by the Scorpion samurai during long campaigns. The vault was now used as a prison for higher-caste criminals with minimum security requirements. This had earned it the name "ji-u," referring to the gracious rain that blessed crops in Ryokō Province; it was a popular pun on "jiyū," the word for freedom.

In addition to the underground vault, the compound had a gravel courtyard that housed a few ancient administrative buildings and another one of Seno's spy-deterring waterfalls. This one was inscribed with the word "Meiyo": Honor, the first precept of Rokugani law, deriving, of course, from the Bushidō tenet. Yojiro could guess that the Ryokō Owari Prison, where Buyu and the Storm Tigers had been taken, had a matching waterfall with the second precept, "Jihaku," the principle of confession, inscribed.

"How long have you been working for Magistrate Otomo?"

"Nearly fifteen years. I was appointed as his yoriki just after my graduation from the Seppun School of Magistrates."

"I have heard that the Seppun train some of the best magistrates when it comes to investigation."

Motome blushed again at the praise. "The school is very good, but you are mistaken in including me among the ranks of great investigators."

"We shall see. Fifteen years' experience is quite the accomplishment."

She smiled. "Perhaps. What about you? How long have you been Emerald Magistrate in Otosan Uchi?"

"Six years."

"So you were appointed by Champion Doji Satsume, then."

Yojiro remembered the late Emerald Champion, the one Toturi had replaced. The old Crane samurai had been strict, devoted. "Yes."

"So both Satsume-sama and Toturi-sama trust you," Motome observed, more to herself than to Yojiro. "Do you have friends?"

Now it was Yojiro's turn to blush. "Friends? Well, I—"

"Oh, curse my curiosity," Motome stuttered, shaking her head as if coming to her senses. She bowed apologetically. "I did not mean to interrogate you. I was…writing your character profile in my head. A matter of habit, I'm afraid. Please forgive me."

"It is quite all right," Yojiro replied, the answers to her questions starting to gnaw inside him. Did he have friends? He spent more time with Lady Kachiko than anyone else, but he would hardly consider her a friend. Their relationship was more…professional? More complicated, anyway. He listed the people at court who were friendly to him.

"I suppose I can consider Toturi-sama my friend," he replied slowly. "We respect one another."

"Yes, I suppose friends should respect one another," Motome said, her smile drooping.

Yojiro frowned. He had not considered it. Besides Mikuru, who would no longer speak to him, he truly had no one. Scorpion were repelled by his honesty, and few others accepted him, because an honest Scorpion was too much of an anomaly. Maybe that was why he spent so much time carving, making trinkets, whittling toys. He was just…alone.

They entered the largest building in the courtyard: a worn, grey outbuilding with the Scorpion crest in ancient, sun-bleached paint above the sliding door. The prickling stench of mildew greeted them, the air musty from the lack of windows. Numerous oil lamps filled the halls and rooms, enough to blind the eye as they rounded corners and to suck the already-stale air out of the rooms. No doubt more of Seno's ingenious schemes to catch ninja.

As they descended a heavy, split-post draw ramp down into the vault, Yojiro crouched slightly to avoid the low ceiling. The cells were made of fist-thick, red-pine lattices, like cages for wild animals, the holes only large enough for an eye to peer through. However, as this prison housed high-ranking, genteel criminals, they were sanitary, even mildly furnished. Beds. Chairs. The occasional desk. Despite the accommodations, Yojiro could see bleak expressions behind the bars. Ministers. Priests. Courtiers. People used to luxuries, who could not appreciate merely a dry bed and a clean floor.

*Why did Aramoro let himself get put into a place like this? Did he and Kachiko plan this?*

His worries gnawed inside him as he and Motome arrived at her office, which she unlocked with a heavy iron key from her brass ring. Despite her rank and ability, Seno had tucked her away in this dungeon, deep within the prison vault. However, she hinted at no irritation at the location. She clearly took care of the tiny room. The walls were crowded with perfectly organized shelves of scrolls and iron-bound chests, not a speck of dust visible.

No tatami mats had been installed, likely due to mold growing in the damp, so Motome set out a pair of lavender *zabuton* pillows for them to kneel upon. Then, carefully, she hung her pair of swords, katana and *wakizashi*, upon a plain wooden rack. Her jitte also went on its own little stand.

"I would offer you some refreshment, but I command no amenities here at this prison," Motome apologized, regret at the social impropriety pinching her eyebrows. "Please forgive me."

"There is nothing to forgive," Yojiro assured her. He first knelt politely in *seiza* position upon the cushion, but she gestured that he could relax.

"I have all the materials from the murder investigation in here," she explained, unlocking a pine chest with a key from her brass ring. She withdrew scrolls, letters, wooden boxes, and even a basket of bloodied clothes from it, setting each article carefully upon her low desk. She watched him with hawkish vigilance, as though afraid he would take something. He ignored her suspicion as he examined the articles.

"Did you collect them yourself? Or did you get them from Captain Denmaru?" Yojiro asked, referring to what Hyobu had said about turning over the case.

Motome's face hardened into a defensive scowl. "Yes, Captain Denmaru gave me some of these articles."

"I did not mean to offend by implying incompetence on your part," Yojiro apologized. "Rather, I heard from Governor Hyobu that he was originally investigating the Kitsuki's death."

"And I was implying…never mind," Motome bit her lip, rethinking her statements. "Captain Denmaru and I have often quarreled. As a representative of the Emerald Magistrate, my attempts to uphold Imperial law sometimes clash with his enforcement of local law. We sometimes have not seen eye to eye in the execution of our duties."

"Confusion in the lines of jurisdiction?"

"More than that," Motome explained. "Sometimes I wonder if he may have purposely hindered some of my investigations."

"This is a grave suspicion, Motome-san. What has given you such an impression?"

"Forgive my directness, Yojiro-sama. In the past, I merely experienced obstacles that have caused me to wonder: untimely arrests of my witnesses, damage to evidence, and killings of my suspects. Many of these instances involved the Thunder Guard in some way. Some of them may have been merely unfortunate accident, but part of me remains skeptical. Otomo-sama has also often protested against Captain Denmaru, having had some of his own efforts obstructed."

"Seemingly obstructed, you mean?"

Motome turned her face away, the shame of her allegations burning across her face. "I am sorry, Yojiro-sama. The only reason I mention this at all is due to our partnership. I have long come to expect interference from Hyobu and her Thunder Guard, and you might need to as well, even if we have no proof."

Motome bit her lip again.

Yojiro sunk down into his high collar to think. The Scorpion carefully trained the Shosuro to work in secret, so the fact that Motome had no proof of whatever she feared did not surprise him. Surely, this was the interference Toturi also feared, probably having heard reports from Seno himself. Yet, despite everyone's suspicions about Hyobu and Denmaru, including his own, Yojiro knew that Motome shared some of Seno's bias against the Scorpion. She was almost aware of it herself, the old Otomo's paranoia undoubtedly making it clearer by the day, but that prejudice was sure to still color her judgment.

*I need to bide my time. Wait. And watch.*

"Thank you, Motome-san," he finally said to repair her embarrassment. "If I have reason to suspect Captain Denmaru, I shall share it with you, as you have found reason to share your inner thoughts with me. Since I am a newcomer, I cannot yet pass any judgments, and I look forward to becoming more acquainted with the facts, as you are."

The yoriki stared at him, astonished at his willingness to ignore her improperly critical outburst. "That is generous of you."

"Not at all," he replied. "We shall proceed as we can, regardless of the obstacles."

Gently, he pulled close some of the articles from her investigation. A large porcelain urn containing Kitsuki Obo's cremated remains, sealed with wax. A yellow silk coin purse with a ragged lining. An ivory case containing Obo's signature chop. A jade ring with a dragon's head etched into its surface. A tiny brass key. Some identification papers speckled with blood. At the bottom of the pile, a few letters of introduction from the appropriate Dragon Clan officials and Kitsuki gold mine owners. He scanned their contents, reading about Obo's duties as one of many trade ministers representing Dragon trade interests in the area.

*These articles give no indication of why the Scorpion would have any interest in him. He seems as powerless and inconsequential as any other low-ranking samurai retainer.*

Yojiro next picked his way through the basket. Obo's kimono was a very simple green and yellow layered garment with no embroidery and only a cotton lining. The sides had been reseamed about a palm's length in from the garment's original width, as if the kimono had previously belonged to a much larger man, becoming a secondhand castoff. Bloodstains followed several tears in the silk, congregating in a pattern. There had been three quick strikes: precise slashes near the neck, belly, and groin. The Swiftness of Shadows Technique. Aramoro's fighting style.

Yojiro's body nearly recoiled from the clothing as though it carried a plague.

Had Aramoro truly killed Obo? If so, then Yojiro would not be determining and sharing the truth, as he had hoped. That would surely lead to the Traitor's Grove. Could that have been Aramoro and Kachiko's plan all along? To use Aramoro's crime to force Yojiro to dishonor himself, anticipating that the truth would force him to lie? It could not be as twisted as that.

He dropped the clothes back into the basket. The garments fell in a way that concealed Aramoro's slash pattern. He gritted his teeth.

*Lies are unnecessary if one can simply speak around the truth.*

"Motome-san, how do you know that Kitsuki-sama received training from the Kitsuki School of Investigators?" Yojiro asked, trying to ignore his subconscious deception.

Motome sat back on her cushion, her slight wince indicating that Obo's loss had not been painless.

"I first met Kitsuki-sama about ten years ago at a tavern in the North Rim neighborhood in Fishers' Quarter. I was there investigating burglaries. He heard that I was Otomo-sama's personal yoriki and approached me, asking me to help him. He seemed somewhat unnerved. Frantic, really. He told me someone was following him. Trying to kill him. He kept looking over his shoulder and seemed scared of his own shadow."

"Those sentiments seem natural here in Ryokō Owari," Yojiro observed. "I felt that same disorientation when I arrived earlier today. Otomo-sama's own fear has seems to have blossomed from a similar effect."

"No, this was different. Kitsuki-sama kept muttering strange nonsense about shinobi. Roof climbers. Ambushes. Poison. Assassins. At first, I thought he was merely a raving drunkard, but he showed me a piece of paper with a strange symbol on it, a kind of serpentine pattern of knotted strokes and crescents." Motome hesitated a moment to stare at Yojiro with her honey-colored eyes. After a deep breath to clear the suspicion wrinkled in her forehead, she continued. "He told me that the picture was a dark Scorpion secret, something he would be killed for if the Scorpion knew he had it. I was still unsure, but he kept repeating himself in such incredible earnest. That I needed to help him. That he was not safe. I told him we could talk when he was sober, hoping he would make more sense later, so I left him overnight.

"The next morning, I visited the inn where he was staying, a place called the Fortuitous Wind. He did not quite remember me, probably due to the drunkenness. I repeated what he had told me the night before, the story about the Scorpion killing him, and he denied that too. He only acknowledged that I spoke the truth after I mentioned his drawing of that strange symbol. He invited me in and confessed that he had been sent to Ryokō Owari by his masters at the Kitsuki School of Investigation to observe covert Scorpion activity. Anything illegal or incriminating."

"How do you know that he was telling the truth?"

"He showed me his secret identification papers and his instructions from the investigator school. They were signed by the Kitsuki family daimyō."

"Do you have those documents here?"

"No; they were not on his person when he died," Motome explained, somewhat defiantly in the face of Yojiro's question. "But I am sure we can find them if we search his room at the inn. Otomo-sama has yet to sign a search warrant for me. He has been busy with other investigations."

*Oh yes, the dangerous Storm Tiger ninja gang.*

"Anyway, when Kitsuki-sama showed me those documents, he said that he had started to gather information regarding Scorpion shinobi. My reaction to him was similar to yours. I laughed at him and went back to thinking that perhaps this was just some joke or hallucinatory ravings. Even with all the crime here in Ryokō Owari, I could not believe that the samurai of a Great Clan would flagrantly violate the Imperial edict that forbids the use of shinobi. But he said that he was not a liar, just as earnestly I insisted that to you, Yojiro-sama. He asked if I would help him."

"And you said you would?"

"This was about the time when Otomo-sama developed an interest in ninja activity. He had mentioned seeing spies inside the manor, which spurred his fierce campaigns against them. I thought that by helping Kitsuki-sama, I could help Otomo-sama's efforts as well. So, I told Kitsuki-sama I would."

"Did he ever explain what the strange symbol was?" Yojiro asked, almost more confused by the story than enlightened. What strange Scorpion secrets had the two of them stumbled upon?

"He said something about a coded picture. An image that the shinobi could use to leave messages in plain sight for each other. I think it looked more like a tattoo. However, I could be mistaken. I only saw it once. In fact, I did not see Kitsuki-sama again after that day, owing to the secrecy of our missions. He did keep in contact, however, sending me messages every few months hidden in my packages from my laundress." Motome opened a small wooden box that contained dozens of slips of paper no wider than her little finger. Yojiro selected a handful and scanned their contents.

"Scouted Blossom Dock. Followed but lost him at the Bay of Drowned Honor.

"Counted four, maybe five, potential suspects while watching Alabaster Street. Talking about poisoned opium.

"Gathering planned. Rooftop of Temple of Amaterasu. Date undetermined. Will observe the area.

"Shadows sighted. Iron Wharf. Hour of the Ox. Escaped again."

The rest of them were similar. Places. Times. Shadows and rumors from all over the city, every one eluding Obo's firm grasp. There were no real patterns, no linked facts, no actual substantive accomplishments. In fact, Yojiro saw no real evidence of shinobi in the messages, only reports so vague that they stunk of a productive incompetence, much like Seno's own ninja-hunting activities. The bumbling reports of a man pretending to work.

However, another possibility surfaced as Yojiro read through more of them, remembering Motome's story about a drunk, paranoid Kitsuki investigator afraid of his own shadow, afraid of death. Perhaps chasing ghosts had twisted Obo, goading him to obsessively attempt to prove the impossible: that shinobi exist. His shame and fear of the truth, perhaps, had driven him to paranoia and delusion. Maybe Motome's naïve, conveniently timed faith in his story had reset his deluding self-assurances.

Yojiro looked over the slips again, noting the careful handwriting, Motome's added dates on the backs, the chop marks that matched Obo's signature. The only glimmer of proof that shinobi existed was Motome's mention of the painting Obo had showed her at their first meeting. If only Yojiro could find it, or someone who might know about it.

"Thank you for sharing this with me, Motome-san," Yojiro said, helping her return the evidence back to the chest. "Please excuse my continued skepticism of the shinobi component. These slips are an interesting collection, but I think that perhaps they need to be sorted to make more sense to my slow sensibilities. Maybe we will find something more obvious after we search Kitsuki-sama's apartment. In the meantime, I think it is time to move on to Aramoro-sama's involvement."

"Of course. I will arrange for an interrogation immediately." She handed him a scroll before rising and rushing to the door. "This report details what I have found thus far that implicates Aramoro-sama in the death of Kitsuki Obo."

A half hour later, Yojiro pinched his lips to smother a weak, watery unease that was creeping into his chest as the guards led Aramoro into the interrogation room. The accused killer's cruel mouth dangled in a mocking smile, a perversion of the oni mask that usually covered the bottom half of his face. Yojiro dared not look away.

"It is good to see you again, Aramoro-sama," he began.

"Yes, it is." Aramoro snickered, dark humor painting his sharp eyes. "The honest Scorpion descends to the City of Lies. Good indeed."

"I come at the command of the Emerald Champion to aid in investigating your involvement in the issue at hand."

"If that's what you believe…" Aramoro trailed off, his leer deepening. "Where's the Seppun woman?"

"Since her report said you were rather quiet during her interviews with you, I suggested that you might say more without her here."

"Fine." Without taking his eyes off of Yojiro, he addressed the guards. "You may leave us. I have much to discuss with my fellow Scorpion."

Yojiro nodded at the order, a bit unnerved that Aramoro so smoothly assumed command over everyone around him, even when he was in chains. The guards sidled out, brusquely barring the heavy door behind them to lock the two Scorpion in. Aramoro slumped himself down onto his zabuton, refusing to bend his knees in polite seiza. Yojiro ignored it.

"I have a few questions to ask you," he began. "I would like to hear your version of the events behind Kitsuki Obo's dea—"

"You know, I talked to your sister just before I left Otosan Uchi," Aramoro interrupted, chuckling. "Do you know what she called you, Yojiro? After the tournament?"

"That does not concern our present topic—"

"She called you a lapdog to a lion. One with an emerald collar. Is that not a delightful picture? So fierce."

Yojiro ignored the provocation. "Why are you here in Ryokō Owari? I was not aware that Lord Shoju gave you freedom to travel."

"I wouldn't call this freedom," Aramoro snapped, swishing a finger around to point at the thick walls. "No air. Too much light from these damned lanterns. Half-wit sentries to watch me sleep and piss."

"As far as I am aware, you have not been mistreated while in Otomo Seno-sama's custody."

"I wasn't mistreated until they locked me up with you, you servile worm."

Yojiro frowned.

"Yes, you would be the one Toturi would pick," Aramoro grumbled, still enjoying the power of his jabs. "You're so honorable. So…trustworthy."

Aramoro's bitterness recalled the Tournament of the Emerald Champion, and Yojiro stiffened inside his high collar.

*Does Aramoro know I warned Toturi?*

He attempted to fathom a spark of knowledge inside Aramoro's reddened eyes but only saw the samurai making his own calculations.

*No. He's searching me, too. He only suspects. How could someone so alert allow himself to get caught?*

"Why are you in this city, Aramoro-sama?"

"To suffer my humiliating defeat in exile, of course. I fled Otosan Uchi for my reputation's sake. If I must hide, why not crawl into the cave with the best pleasure courts in Rokugan in it?"

"And how do you account for your involvement in Kitsuki Obo's murder?"

"Bad fortune," Aramoro said, obviously amused. "We were guests at the same inn. He ended up dead, and it seems his bad luck is trying to drag me down with him. Perhaps I have not been saying enough prayers to Fukurokujin for daily deliverance."

"Did you know him?"

"No."

"Motome-san's report indicates several witnesses saw you speaking with the Kitsuki the day before he was found dead in the street."

Aramoro smiled, his angular teeth glistening in the lamplight. "Bad fortune, indeed."

"Her report also suggests that your clothes had blood on them."

"A shaving accident."

"As you are the Whisper of Steel, a shaving accident seems unlikely," Yojiro said, growing tired and angry at the samurai's deflections. Aramoro was obviously lying, but Yojiro could not tell if he was lying for the sake of the clan or out of spite. Either way, his lies were an unnecessary obstacle. "Aramoro-sama, an honest answer from you would make my duties much easier."

Suddenly, Aramoro's face hardened into a frightening scowl. "Is that why you fail at your duty? Because you think it should be easy? No, Yojiro. Betrayal is easy. And you are lower than selfish swine spit if you believe you are superior to those of us who sacrifice everything for the clan."

This stung more than all of Aramoro's past insults. No matter how he defended the actions he had taken during the Tournament of the Emerald Champion, the Scorpion would only ever see it as disloyalty. He had undone their treachery, but he had also slighted their Mother of Scorpions with his failure.

Yojiro stood, rising above Aramoro's cheap blows, and knocked on the door to signal the guards to unlock it. "I will return when you are ready to talk, Aramoro-sama."

He left the room without a second glance. Motome stood outside, waiting for him, holding an armful of writing utensils for composing a report about his conversation with Aramoro.

"Did he tell you anything useful?" she asked. "Or did he just laugh in your face like he did to me?"

Yojiro stared at Motome a moment, relief unknotting his stomach. During the last several hours, working with this Seppun yoriki had been so simple compared to the layers of tricks, feints, and plots inherent in dealing with his own clan. Aramoro. Hyobu and Denmaru. Even the pathetic Ikku demanded precautions, discernments, wary responses. He smiled. For the first time, it seemed, he knew what trust felt like.

# Chapter Five

*Y*ojiro returned to the estate of the Emerald Magistrate the next day to ask Seno for the search warrant. Motome was already in the waterfall courtyard. She crouched, almost in a combat stance, fierce anger contorting her face. The old Emerald Magistrate took no notice as he studied several thick scrolls stacked upon his tiny bamboo desk.

"Ah, Bayushi-sama," Seno sneered over the loudness of the falling water. "You are just in time. I was just telling Motome-san that the Storm Tigers have confessed their despicable crimes."

"Those fools admitted to being ninja?" Yojiro asked, incredulous. Under the law, if they gave verbal testimony, they could be condemned and punished, even if no physical evidence could be found to prove their guilt.

"Yes, finally. They were loath to relinquish their wicked secrets, but my perseverance was rewarded after I sent an interrogator."

"They confessed under torture?"

"And now he is planning their executions!" Motome shouted. Had there been no waterfall, she might have been reprimanded for defiance. Her eyes pleaded with Yojiro, the shame of her participation smoldering inside of her.

"There is no precedent in our archives for how ninja ought to be executed," Seno said, ignoring Motome and scouring his law scrolls. "However, I think boiling them alive might be just."

"No," Yojiro argued. "You cannot do this."

"Bayushi-sama," Seno snapped, his bony face growing gaunter with indignation. He folded his arms, glaring at the Scorpion magistrate. "These criminals are under my jurisdiction, so I shall be their judge. You have no control over anything in this city except for that pathetic investigation Toturi-sama allows you to play with. You would do well to remember this."

Lightning fast, Yojiro raced through the situation in his mind. Buyu and the others were not ninja. Merely ruffians. Seno's obsession had stretched too far. Executing them for worse crimes than their own would be a grave injustice, a mockery of the law.

*But I will gain no ground fighting him. In fact, I may lose it if, in his rage, he refuses to issue our search warrant. My first duty is to uncover Obo's secrets, for my clan. However, Bushidō demands I fight to prevent this injustice, and as his equal in rank, only I can.*

"Otomo-sama," Yojiro began, selecting his words with the utmost care. He could not afford the convenient slip of a lie with Motome watching. "I am afraid that in my haste, I did not communicate myself well. Please forgive me."

"Oh?" Seno said, his chin wrinkled with bitterness.

"Yes, I did not intend to defy your prerogative or your power over this city. As Emerald Magistrate of Ryokō Owari, you have Heaven's blessing to enforce and judge the sacred laws of our land here. I simply thought that perhaps, since this is an exceptional situation, you should inform Toturi-sama of your achievement first. After all, no Emerald Magistrate has successfully captured ninja in eight or nine centuries. He may want to inspect your prisoners before you execute them."

Seno stroked the black hair on his chin, pondering, though suspicions of the Scorpion's supposition. "What trick are you playing, Bayushi-sama?"

"No trick, Otomo-sama. I merely present the possible consequences of your success. Toturi-sama may want to make an example of you and your efforts for other magistrates."

"Yojiro-sama is right, Otomo-sama," Motome added, catching

on to his ploy and adding to the bait. She knelt before Seno in humble supplication. "Please allow me to write a letter to Toturi-sama, telling him of our accomplishment here."

"No. I shall write the letter of my accomplishment," Seno asserted, greedy excitement causing his hands to tremble. "Yes, Toturi-sama will want to hear of my victory for justice. Such important news surely will interest him."

Moments later, Seno scraped an inkstick into an enormous black puddle on his inkstone for a long letter while Motome and Yojiro left, bearing away their search warrant.

"Thank you," Motome muttered. Despite their success in saving the Storm Tigers, her voice was low, soft with dejection, her warm eyes wet with a repentant sorrow. "How foolish I was. My part in this wretched business was dishonorable."

"You obeyed your lord, loyally fulfilling your duty, Motome-san," Yojiro reassured her.

"Yes, but I defied his judgment, his authority. I was so afraid of my mistake that I became a disobedient servant. I fought against my master."

"But your compassion and integrity were noble..." Yojiro stopped. His tongue grew leaden. She had done exactly what he had done to Kachiko, and she longed for reprimand. They both defied their masters' authority, seeking to undo their personal mistakes. Motome to save the Storm Tigers a cruel fate. Yojiro for his own honor. They had righted the treacherous wrongs of their masters, but was there dishonor in such disobedience? Were there karmic consequences for defying even a wicked lord?

*Was Aramoro right? Am I merely justifying my disloyalty? Motome is prepared to sacrifice her honor for Seno. Am I not willing to sacrifice myself for my clan? To suffer for duty?*

Yojiro winced at the implications. He had considered himself selfless, righteous, pure. But now, he could see the stain upon his skin that Aramoro had spat upon, the one that disgusted Kachiko. He shook his head. *Can I be just and a Scorpion at the same time?*

In spite of his initial hesitation, Yojiro and Motome rode a rickshaw to the Fishers' Quarter to find the inn where Obo had spent the last twelve years. The Fortuitous Wind, a derelict two-story guesthouse, squatted inside a back alley near the docks. Generations of dead fish and unbathed fisherfolk had pressed their oily scent into every board and brick, and the gutters along the alley ran brown with constant trickles of fish guts draining into the Bay of Drowned Honor. The entire district was nearly black as dusk that morning, the sky engulfed in the reeking smoke from innumerable cooking fires and smokehouses. Sailors, butchers, vendors, smokers, and cooks scuttled past to process their catches before rot sank in.

Surely a Dragon Clan gold trader could afford better accommodations. Especially if he really was funded by the Kitsuki School of Investigation. Why did Obo choose to live here? Was the location inconspicuous? Closer to shinobi activity?

The last thought made him laugh at himself.

*You are starting to sound like Seno.*

Outside the inn, a few filthy urchins played in the street puddles. They eyed Motome but thought better of throwing sludge balls when they saw Yojiro.

*They must know not to disturb a well-dressed Scorpion.*

"I need to go speak with another witness to finish my report," Motome mumbled, pointing to a man across the alleyway smoking grey squid over a filthy brick oven. "Go show the innkeeper our warrant, and I will meet you in there."

Yojiro lingered a moment as Motome crossed the street, watching her engage the fish smoker. He seemed shy, almost unwilling to speak to her, so she loosened her purse and dropped a few coins into his hand. She saw Yojiro still standing there, so she waved him away, turning back to the laborer.

It seemed a little strange that she suddenly trusted him enough to be autonomous. Was it a show of faith? What were they talking about?

Yojiro slid open the door of the Fortuitous Wind and stepped inside. He only had a moment to dodge a filthy dishrag that splatted against the wall near his head. His hand whipped to his katana, silencing a chorus of accompanying guffaws. A roomful of wide-eyed sailors stared back at him, guilt freezing their faces at their mistake. Seeing Yojiro's fine silk, they crumpled back into private conversations, cautiously eyeing the spot where he stood.

"Oh no!" an old man shouted, running and smearing the greasy smudge on the wall with another rag. He could barely hide an overly playful grin at his joke, even if it had gone amiss. He jumped up and down, trying to mop up the final slimy spot. "Forgive me, sir! We thought that Ebi-kun was back for more!"

The room buzzed with nervous laughter. The sailors were crowded around tables in the small common room, drinking weak sake and sour tea from chipped cups. The walls had other oily splatters, and the floor slipped beneath his sandals, which he dared not remove at the door. Juniper-scented oil lamps sat smoking everywhere, trying vainly to stave off the smell of fish, turning the air thick and gracelessly pungent.

The old man, still giggling to himself, skipped past Yojiro to finish his table rounds with a teapot. He wore a cloth cap over his balding head, liver spots freckled his face, and he boasted but a few teeth, browned with age. Despite his many years, the man's back was unbent, his gait spry.

"Excuse me, Uncle," Yojiro addressed him, assuming he was the proprietor of the inn. "Forgive my intrusion. I have come as a representative of the Emerald Magistrate."

"The Emerald Magistrate?" the old man gasped, a gnarled hand rising to his mouth. His melodramatic tone sounded flippant. "What does old man Otomo want here?"

Yojiro's brow furrowed. As a samurai, he had never been addressed with such boldness from a peasant, let alone one who would casually refer to a superior with such nonchalance and disrespect. In fact, Yojiro did not know old men of any class who talked like that.

"I have a search warrant to inspect the room formerly tenanted by Kitsuki Obo."

"Obo-sama? But what would you want with—ah! Ebi-kun!" The old man squealed. A young man entered wearing a fisherman's short *kosode* and a black scarf looped around his neck. The owner flung the dishrag anew, joined by several sailors throwing rubbish or hats or cups. However, the target merely darted aside and between them with unusual dexterity, the articles splattering and smashing to the floor. The room again filled with roars of amusement.

"You need a new game, Jin-sama," the young man scolded, shaking his head, though a silent delight colored his dark eyes. "I win again."

"No, no, no," the old man Jin nagged. "We will hit you one of these days, Ebi-kun. You are such a cheat!"

More mannerisms that ill-befitted his age emerged in the old man with Ebi's entrance. A delicate wrist flick with the teapot. A sway to the hips. A flirtatious eye.

Yojiro interrupted their conversation, grasping the innkeeper's soft arm gently. "Excuse me, Jin-san."

"What do you want?" Ebi demanded, coming close, nearly springing between the two of them in defense.

"He comes from the Emerald Magistrate," Jin explained hurriedly, waving his hand to calm Ebi. "Here to talk about Obo-sama. No need to worry. I will take care of it."

Both Jin and Ebi referred to the Kitsuki by his first name. So, they knew him well.

The fisherman stood down but kept mistrustful eyes fixed on Yojiro. He sat down at a nearby table and began whispering with the sailors.

"Perhaps we can talk in another room, somewhere more private," Yojiro suggested, pointing to the sliding doors of the back rooms.

Jin nodded, sharing a final, wary glance with Ebi before leading the way. "Of course. Please follow me."

They went into a tiny storeroom stuffed with rank futon mattresses and cheap linens, a tiny window netted with cobwebs admitting the only light. Yojiro shut the door behind them. Jin shrank into the corner, growing somewhat shy, rubbing his hands together and biting his lip.

"Forgive my eagerness," Yojiro began, quite sure of his deduction now. Jin was not a man but a woman. A young woman. "I have serious business I would like to conduct in your fine establishment. It is yours, is it not?"

"Oh yes, it is." Jin's demure unease made her previous caprice all the more telling.

"Well, you seem to care for it with such youthful vigor," Yojiro said pointedly. "However, I am sure that since you do not see many of my rank or status here often, you might be concerned to know that your...performance of duty toward me was somewhat lacking. An earnest member of your station would do well to remember differences of class conduct and act accordingly."

Jin had started to sweat tiny drops, but a childish pride was also beginning to harden her jaw. "You…observe well."

"And, if I might add one more piece of advice," Yojiro continued. "A man, especially a man of venerable years, ought to act with more dignity when in the presence of young, handsome men. I have never seen old men tease quite as you do, and I cannot say I find it appropriate for your role."

"I understand your meaning," Jin said, sulkily, as a child caught stealing pressed-sugar candy. "You honor me with the lesson. I shall…act, as you say, more in line with my age, station, and gender."

"I might suggest spending more time with aged men, to learn their ways."

Jin smiled, that flirtatious sparkle lighting up the eyes again. "Are you volunteering to show me those ways?"

Yojiro grinned. "I am not that old."

"Of course not. Old men never think they are when in the right company."

Yojiro smiled and bowed to the young woman, a small respect for her growing. She was an excellent Soshi shugenja. Her illusion had been quite good with its extreme attention to detail, tricking even him at first. However, her poor acting had shattered that mask far too easily. Still in training, perhaps, making the innkeeper Jin a practice role. She must have a clever sensei. An inn constantly full of strangers made for a perfect training ground, where mistakes and inconsistencies might pass unnoticed.

"Now, to business," he continued, showing her his magisterial identification papers and search warrant. "I am Bayushi Yojiro, Emerald Magistrate from Otosan Uchi. I come not only on behalf of the Emerald Champion himself but also on behalf of Governor Hyobu to work with local authorities in investigating Kitsuki Obo-sama's death."

"I see," the young woman said, still in her old man's voice, though it had deepened somewhat with an anxious guilt.

"Did you get to know him well while working here?"

"Yes…" The shugenja trailed off, growing graver at the question. "In a way."

"What way?"

Before she could answer, the door suddenly slid open, and Ebi, a suspicious glower marring his face, marched into their small meeting space. He strode directly between them, hiding the young woman behind him.

"Someone is here to see you, sir," he said, pointing back out in the common room at Motome.

"There you are, Yojiro-sama," the Seppun samurai said. Her eyebrows arched at finding them in a closet, but she held her tongue. "Shall we inspect Kitsuki-sama's room?"

Yojiro nodded, stepping out. The false Jin gave them a key and directions to Obo's apartment before returning to her customers, this time more carefully hunching her back and hobbling her step.

As they walked toward the stairs to the second floor, Motome touched Yojiro's arm lightly. "Did you notice anything strange about that young fisherman?" she whispered.

"Beyond his marvelous reflexes and irritability, no," Yojiro confessed, creasing his brow. "What did you see?"

"Nothing really," she confessed. "Except that he is the cleanest fisherman I ever saw. He doesn't even stink."

Yojiro looked over his shoulder back at Ebi, who still fixed a sharp glare upon him. As far as Yojiro could tell, the man wore no illusion. However, he was missing the calluses on his hands that came from the constant wear of rope and net. He was also not nearly as sun scorched as the other fisherfolk and sailors in the common room.

*How odd. Jin. Ebi. Obo. Three people under one roof with secret selves...*

"What did your witness across the street say?" Yojiro asked as they found Obo's room and entered using the key. The cramped chamber, though significantly cleaner than the rest of the Fortuitous Wind, had mold-soiled tatami mats and a narrow sliding window. A fine layer of dust and stray soot from outside coated the chest of drawers, desk, and folded futon. No one had been in here in weeks.

"He said he had seen the Kitsuki many times over the last ten years," answered Motome, taking note of the furnishings, careful not to disturb too much yet. "They never spoke, but he said there were neighborhood rumors about why he had decided to live in North Rim instead in the Merchant Quarter like the other trade ministers.

Something about associating with street orphans who eventually were never seen again. As far as I can tell, it was merely vulgar gossip."

"Are you sure?" Yojiro asked. Every new detail about this man was stranger than the last. "What if he were a child stealer?"

Motome's face grew steely, her thin lips quivering in a sudden rage. "Street children disappear all the time, and do you know who is to blame? Scorpion crime lords. Scorpion toughs. They have sucked this city's marrow to dust. Opium eaters. Thieves. Whoremongers. Living in this wretched city has showed me to what depraved depths your clan's lies and manipulations sink. And when someone tries to stop you, to loosen some of your choke-holds around our throats, they end up dead!"

Her unexpected outburst ended as quickly as it had sprung. She looked away, her cheeks crimson in embarrassment. Yojiro stood, uneasily watching as the tense moment stretched into silence. He sunk behind his collar.

Was this a distraction? An emotional attempt at changing the subject? She had wanted to talk to the fish smoker in private, so perhaps she was hiding what their conversation had truly been about. He tried to read her body to confirm, but the stiff shoulders angled away from him, and her sinking jaw spoke of pain. Her posture huddled around her heart.

"Motome-san," he started, unsure of what to say. He swallowed.

"Forgive me," Motome muttered, squeezing the handle of her jitte with a shaking fist. "That witness went missing the day Oto-mo-sama assigned me to take over the case from Captain Den-maru. Another inconvenient obstruction. I was angry. Now, being in Kitsuki-sama's room reminds me too much…of how I must now do all this alone. The loss of a comrade-in-arms against this dark, lying city is difficult."

Yojiro's first instincts were to lie, to attempt to save face for his clan, but there was no point in defending his clan in light of her experience. Ryokō Owari Toshi was plagued by all that she said it was. In fact, he was there to be part of it. Kachiko had made sure of that. In the end, no matter how much he wanted to be honest with Motome—as honest as she ever had been with him, even to her humiliation—no matter how conflicted he was in his soul, he would need to race her to the truth, to absolve Aramoro by any means necessary, to hide any hint of Scorpion guilt. He knew he would be forced to betray her.

*I can only commit to tell her the truth where I can. No more.*

"You know, Motome-san," he started again, his heart still heavy. He looked her straight in the eyes and tempered his voice to an even pitch, just as any good liar is trained to. "I am on your side."

Her chin tightened as her teeth ground together. She let out a strained breath, and her cheeks softened as she relented.

"Perhaps," she muttered, turning her back to him. "We shall see."

Together, they made a careful dissection of the room. The drawers were stuffed with many sets of used kimono, all altered to fit, like Obo's death clothes had been. They also found a shaving mirror and razor, several pairs of geta with worn soles, small jars of medicinal ointment, and a volume of the *Tao of Shinsei*, bound in green and yellow silk—Dragon colors. The pages felt crisp the spine was unstretched.

The only other bit of furniture was a magnolia-wood desk with a deep red lacquer finish. Not quite master grade, but clever work. The legs were fashioned like the squat claws of a tortoise, the edges etched with wildflowers native to Yuma Province, indicative of Soshi artisans. Though it was not odd for Obo to have had a Scorpion-made desk, as he had been living in a Scorpion city, the uncommon expense of this particular extravagance clashed with his threadbare, secondhand lifestyle. The light yet strong wood of magnolia trees was cultivated exclusively for decorative crafts, making it a costly piece.

*Perhaps this was the only luxury he was allowed. It certainly is only conspicuous to those allowed within this room.*

The drawers were locked, but Motome had brought Obo's tiny brass key, which fit. Despite getting past the locks, the drawers were lodged shut. With a quick jerk, Yojiro wrenched a drawer out, sending papers and brushes bursting onto the floor. Files on gold pricing, scrolls, and loose slips of paper like Motome's messages had been crammed into every space inside the desk, with ink bottles and ragged brushes wedged in between the gaps. Yojiro scanned the mess for the Scorpion symbol Obo had showed Motome at their first meeting. Seeing nothing similar, he fished out a particularly well-worn notebook tucked carefully in the back of one drawer and flipped through the pages. Place names appeared. House of the Plum Blossom, House of the Morning Star, House of Foreign Stories—geisha houses from Ryokō Owari's Licensed Quarter. Next to the locations were names, printed in tiny characters, along with dates scattered over the last ten years.

"It seems our trade minister was a frequenter of pleasure houses," Yojiro said, handing Motome the ledger. "The names of his favored geisha performers, perhaps?"

Motome scanned the lists. "I don't know. We should take all of his documents back to the magistrate's manor so we can reference them against the police archives. There is too much here to properly address in one sitting, anyway."

Yojiro nodded, gathering the papers that had fallen beneath the desk. Crouching beneath, he paused to look for a tradesperson's marking for the piece. The bottom was unmarked by any guild, trade school, or craftsperson. Yojiro froze. Unmarked work often meant secret work. He ran his hand over the smooth grain. As his fingers climbed up the sides, he felt a tiny raised bump. A nearly invisible switch had been fashioned into the side, probably a latch for a false bottom.

Yojiro's heart sank as he stood from beneath the desk.

*A need to lie so soon. Mere moments after my commitment to be honest.*

Motome was bundling the documents into easily transportable packets, oblivious of his discovery. She had been so honest with him, even about her inability to trust him. And she wanted to trust him, even made efforts toward overcoming her reticence, such as granting him private audience with Aramoro as a show of faith. How could he return her efforts with treachery?

His mouth almost opened of its own accord, but he clamped his lips shut, struggling to smother the news.

Kachiko's mournful threat played across his mind again.

*"The Traitor's Grove is such a cold place. I would hate to have to visit you there."*

Failure meant more than death. Failure meant losing his soul. If Obo's desk had been Dragon made, he would not have to hide it. But…this development was too risky a coincidence.

*Perhaps honesty is worth the price. Aramoro spoke of sacrifice for clan loyalty, but perhaps I can make that same sacrifice for... Who am I making this sacrifice for?*

Rokugan. Rokugan was his treasure. The Emperor, his master. If Yojiro were affixed to a tree, he could not defend the Empire. As the only honest Scorpion, there were things only he could do to save it. He could not fail again if he wanted to continue to serve.

He turned his back on the desk and silently unfastened the window before kneeling to help Motome.

*I will come back tonight to open the desk. Alone.*

# Chapter Six

The Hour of the Rat lay silent as Yojiro slipped into the backstreet in the Fishers' Quarter. District lanterns had long been extinguished, and only the occasional feral cat prowled the viscous darkness. The suffocating daytime smoke had died down, letting the stench of fish bloom in the hot night air. The moon glistened in the street slime, and amorphous clouds conjured waxing and waning shapes in the alleys. Yojiro's eyes had grown somewhat accustomed to the shadows, as he had walked in darkness all the way from his room in Shosuro Palace, through the deserted Merchant Quarter, to the North Rim. Worried about a Thunder Guard spy, he had bound his feet with sandal coverings woven from hemp cords to smother the sounds of his footfalls and had covered the glint of his lacquered scabbards with black woolen stockings before sneaking out.

The stinking alleyway beneath Obo's window was narrow enough for Yojiro to climb between the walls, so he pressed one hand and knee against each side, gently easing himself up to the second story. Pushing tightly against either wall, his arms burned, his muscles less limber after years in a magistrate's chair. Inching up between the two buildings, he finally reached the window. He let go of the walls, using only his knees and feet to wedge himself securely in place. His legs trembled with his weight, so he quickly wormed his fingernails into the casement to open it.

The wood squealed. He froze, waiting in silence. Long, heavy minutes passed before he could assure himself that no one heard. Drawing a candle from his sleeve, he ground the wax into the wood channel, working by feel in the darkness. His legs continued to tremble with tension. His breath shortened.

*Bishamon-no-Kami, help me.*

Slowly, he tested the window again. The wood creaked much more quietly. It would have to do. His knees shivered, seizing up. As his legs gave out, Yojiro snapped the window open and leaped into the room. He tumbled lightly across the tatami, landing on his hands and knees. Again he waited, straining against the silence to hear if anyone stirred. Nothing.

He dared to catch his breath and muttered a silent prayer of thanks to the Fortune of Strength, for bolstering him. Adding more wax to the casement, he shut it again, silently.

He used his fire striker to light the candle and crept to the desk. The flame glowed hot in the deep red stain, reflecting his own face as if he were submerged in a pool of blood. He knelt to inspect the secret switch. The craftsman had hidden the tiny button, scarcely larger than a grain of rice, in a swirl of the magnolia, the natural wood lines drawing attention away from it. However, concealment often was not enough to protect secrets. Gingerly, he pressed the switch with the bottom of the candle instead of his finger. As he expected, a short, silver needle emerged, triggered by the pressure, stabbing the wax harmlessly and leaving a milky drop behind.

*Scorpion venom.*

A secret panel dropped from the bottom of the desk, revealing a shallow drawer with an iron ring handle. He grasped it and pulled slowly, listening for any more mechanisms inside that might signal more traps. Nothing more clicked. Inside the drawer lay stacked packets of letters, a black silk-bound book, and Obo's identification stamped by the chop of the Kitsuki family daimyō, which Motome had mentioned before. The letters were addressed to Obo from the Kitsuki School of Investigation and carefully arranged by date. He opened the most recent one, dated only a month before Obo's death.

"Greetings, my pupil. Your last communiqué regarding the illegal activities of these Storm Tigers has been relayed to our superiors. We were worried after hearing rumors that they were mere street toughs, but at your assurance, we have updated our records."

Yojiro shook his head. *The Kitsuki investigators have a reputation for being so precise. How could they be fooled? Was Obo truly a fraud, only chasing phantoms in his delusion, like Seno?*

"We have a new task for you," the letter continued, "one that takes precedence for its danger. Another interesting rumor has come to our attention, one circulating through the Scorpion spy network. Our informant tells us that Soshi Ezo, the shadow master, is still alive, and that he is in Ryokō Owari. If this is true, find him. If he only faked his death ten years ago, then his dangerous art of…"

Yojiro paused, unsure of how to read the next word, having never seen it before. The characters were "shadow" and "form," but that introduced a paradox. Shadows had no form.

*Shadow form? Is it read* kagegata? Kagenari?

"…then his dangerous art of kagenari has been thriving all this time. Do not engage him. He is possibly the most dangerous shinobi the Scorpion have yet produced. Until next month,

"Kitsuki Jusai."

Yojiro's heart stopped, his mind rapidly drawing lines between the letter's implications. He did not know Soshi Ezo, or what a shadow master could possibly be, but if this letter was authentic, then the Kitsuki investigators believed Ezo to be a shinobi. Did this confirm Motome's story? Somehow, they had discovered this from Scorpion spies, which not only meant that the Dragon had infiltrated his clan but that they now assuredly knew that the Scorpion used shinobi.

He scanned the paper, the calligraphy, struggling to find any stroke, any defect that could discredit the letter as a fraud. It did not follow Obo's handwriting, even if disguised. The outside was worn and scuffed, as if the letter had actually been transported a long distance. The paper matched none of the paper found within the desk. The signature? He snatched up Obo's secret identification papers again. The chop marks matched, reading "Kitsuki Jusai, the

Kitsuki family daimyō." Yojiro paled. As an Emerald Magistrate, he had seen this chop mark several times in passing. The letters were genuine.

Yojiro shoved the letter into his pocket, as if burying it could erase the message. But the words echoed inside his skull. Scorpion shinobi. His breath rattled. His clan retained samurai who had abandoned the laws of Bushidō.

*What else did Kachiko not tell me? Does she even know?*

Yojiro grasped the notebook bound in black silk, thumbing through the pages. These seemed to be Obo's investigation notes, charting his efforts from the day he arrived until his death, a span of twelve years. Settling into this new, dark city. Exploring the different districts, particularly the Merchant Quarter with its blatant crime. Observing the hierarchies of street and firefighter gangs contending with each other and bribing the Thunder Guard. Meeting and judging Otomo Seno as a capable though unwise magistrate. Locating the opium dens sanctioned by Hyobu. Yojiro hovered over the pages near the time when Obo first met and started working with Motome ten years ago.

"The shadows move without the flicker of flames," Obo had written, his characters large and unbalanced—wild, even. "There are eyes in all the alleys. I turn corners, footfalls promising me someone is there, but no one ever is. Ever since I left that wicked temple, they have followed me. These moving, stalking, suffocating shadows! It's this city! This lying city with its festering sores! It's to blame. This lying city will be my death."

The words sounded like Yojiro's own terror of Ryokō Owari from yesterday. Shapes and shades fooling the eyes, the mind conjuring faces for the silhouettes, never knowing if someone was following. From the sound of it, Obo must have been hallucinating, seeing shinobi in every shadow. Yojiro turned the page to the next entry.

"I will now be working with Seppun Motome, yoriki to Seno," the log read, the handwriting suddenly calmer, returning to its tight, careful characters. "She is driven by ethics, not as perceptive as she thinks, too eagerly dazzled by hope's bright star. Her connection to Seno may prove useful."

Yojiro blinked, reading the notes again. Something had changed. He searched for the root of a torn page, but there was none. Obo had simply moved on, his paranoia cured. He scanned pages again. He was missing something.

*What changed after Obo met Motome?*

The faint hiss of a dagger was Yojiro's only warning.

He flung himself back, away from the downward thrust aimed for his head. His fumbling feet caused him to drop the candle and book, and the darkness splashed thick around him, rippling with his fear as he drew his wakizashi with hot fingers. He couldn't remember the last time he had wielded a blade in defense of his life. It slipped in his hands.

*Calm yourself! Listen. Act!*

His anxious commands crowded his reaction time. A smooth stroke to his left shredded his kimono, and Yojiro only had a moment to flinch before his legs danced away in a half-remembered fighting reflex. The wind of another blow sliced toward his right side, and he caught his enemy's blade with his own, scratching up a vain illumination of sparks.

*My luck won't last. I must leave now!*

Leaping away from his assailant, he tumbled toward the window, but his opponent had anticipated his move and stood there, already waiting.

*He's too fast!*

Yojiro sprang to the door, fumbling with the lock only a moment before flinging open the shōji screen to reveal the burst of moonlight in the hall. A second assailant leaped from behind the puddle of light, crashing into Yojiro, who barely lifted his weapon in time to block a heart-aimed slash. The force shoved him back. Yojiro flinched, waiting for a blow from his rearward attacker. But it never came. The space behind him was empty.

He dared not wait at the mercy of two attackers, so Yojiro ducked beneath the dagger of his forward foe into the hall and bounded toward the stairs. He had only just leaped down a few steps before a jolt on the stairs below divulged the presence of a third attacker, rushing up to meet him. He skittered back up the steps, avoiding four sharp thrusts, the last of which slammed into the wood near his foot. He instinctively kicked the blade away, which clanged down into the dark, and he launched himself straight into his attacker's body.

His body slam met with empty air. He toppled down the rest of the stairs with a crash, knocking the wind from himself. The blood pounded in his ears, and he shook his head to clear it, hoping to catch a hint of the three attackers. Through the flood of adrenaline, he could only make out the light footfalls of a single one.

*Where did the others go?*

Yojiro bounded to his feet, circling away from the sound. However, the sound leaped, as if by echo, from before him to behind him, and Yojiro had to dive forward to avoid a blow to his back.

*Impossible. How can he move through me like a ghost?*

A chill curled behind Yojiro's eyes before plunging deep into his stomach as he remembered Obo's letter from his sensei.

*Kagenari. Shadow taking form.*

His opponent could move in the darkness, melting into the very shadows as through a doorway, only to reemerge in another place, another patch of black, in an instant to catch him at the right place.

*I need light!*

He sped into the common room, straining to hear to give himself an instant's notice. Nearly knocking over the table, he seized an oil lamp, and with fumbling fingers attempted to light it. A tickle of body heat flared behind him, and Yojiro rolled forward over the tabletop, dropping the lamp with a crash. He flung himself to another table, hitting his fire striker in an instant and lighting a new lamp. The flame danced for one moment before Yojiro dashed it to the floor, igniting the spilled juniper oil.

The shadows scattered, wavering across the room as the fire sputtered, giving the shadow-walker no clear paths. A black-swathed man stood opposite Yojiro, retrieved dagger in hand. Though his face was covered, surprise flickered in his eyes.

*My chance!*

Yojiro sprang, switching his wakizashi for his katana in a lightening-swift stroke, the larger chamber giving him more space to move. He slashed at his attacker, aiming for his head. The shinobi ducked, tumbling forward to fight at closer range with his dagger. However, Yojiro was ready, dropping his sword to the floor to catch the man's arm as it swept upward toward his belly. He twisted to the side, avoiding the blade and tearing the man's sleeve. Yojiro whipped the cloth down the arm, tangling the dagger and the man's wrist with the torn rags. The naked arm had a strange scar running down the sun-bronzed skin of the upper bicep. There was a pattern, almost like words, serpentine with pointed arcs all along it, as if it were a kind of message branded onto the flesh. Yojiro, snapping the shinobi's wrist down toward the floor, drew his wakizashi to lop off his attacker's head.

Suddenly, Jin the innkeeper appeared, brandishing a *tantō* knife. Her liver-spotted old-man face knotted in determined anger, she thrust at Yojiro's side. Forced to dodge, he redirected his death blow and swung again, preparing this time to slice them both in half. At the same time, she kicked out at Yojiro's hand, releasing his grip on the shadow-walker, who untangled his wrist and freed his dagger. They ducked beneath Yojiro's blow. The innkeeper then leaped between them, crouching into a defensive stance and shielding the shadow-walker with her body, her *tantō* gleaming in the firelight.

Breathing hard, she nodded to Yojiro, a pleading gesture of good faith.

"Yojiro-sama," she panted.

He hesitated. She swallowed hard and muttered something beneath her breath. Suddenly, her old man's visage melted in the firelight, the illusion falling away as she released her invocation. Her smooth, round cheeks emerged from the gaunt, yellow face, and dewy eyes sparkled past the innkeeper's cloudy, wrinkled ones. A long ponytail swung from the back of her head.

She slowly spun, turning her back to Yojiro to face his attacker, and pointed her blade at him.

"Takao," she whispered, her real voice high and melodic. "Do not kill him."

"Move out of the way, Aoi," Takao hissed, raising his dagger against her. "He has seen too much."

The fire still blazed around them, keeping Yojiro safe from the shadows for the moment, but to be sure, he backed up carefully into the wall, leaving no space for a surprise attack.

"Perhaps he can help us. We are all alone. Sensei's other students have all fled, abandoning us. We need support from our clan. Better yet, Yojiro-sama is the Emerald Magistrate from Otosan Uchi."

Rage flooded the young man's eyes. "Aramoro came from Otosan Uchi too, Aoi. They must have worked together to kill sensei! Don't you see? The clan cares nothing about us."

Yojiro balked at Takao's claim. Obo was their sensei? What was a Dragon Clan samurai doing training Scorpion Clan students? The tangle of revelations left no time to unravel all the threads.

"I did not work with Aramoro," Yojiro explained. "I was sent here to investigate Kitsuki-sama's death. To find out what happened to him. If you know, please tell me. I can only help you if I understand."

"See, Takao? He is here to aid us. We must turn to the clan. We cannot do this alone."

But Takao shook his head. "If you want to spare him, you tell him nothing," he warned, tucking his dagger into a cloth sheath at his side. "As the only remaining senior student of our school, I command it."

Aoi opened her mouth again but, out of respect for Takao, her elder, said nothing. The young couple stared at one another, silence stretching between them. Finally, she nodded, looking apologetically at Yojiro.

"I am sorry, Yojiro-sama. This is our secret."

She went into the back room and returned with a bucket of sand to spread all over the fire. As the grit smothered the flames, darkness returned. In the dimness, Yojiro thought he saw Takao wrap his arm around Aoi's waist.

"Do not return here, Yojiro," Takao said, his words tight with anger. "Or my duty will be to kill you."

The couple left the room, going upstairs to Obo's quarters. Yojiro heard them shuffle through the desk for a moment, and then all was silent. Yojiro exhaled as though he had been holding his breath through the entire ordeal. His body still quivered with adrenaline, his arms and legs hot from battle but his face numb. He had survived. Thank the gods.

Yojiro recovered his katana from the floor and lumbered out the front door. The moon sparkled on its blade, illuminating the dark alley with a tiny spark. To have let it touch the ground, especially that filthy floor in there, had been disrespectful to the ancestors who had wielded it before him. However, the necessary move had saved his life. Another enigma.

*Should I be punished for this as well?*

The conflict was eternal.

He looked up, his eyes again unused to the dark. The world was black. The darkness, a wall for Yojiro. A path for Takao. Kagenari. Shadow taking form. Honor. Dishonor. Lies. Truth. Yojiro felt as if his body were bound up, restricted in all ways, a hundred million filaments constricting his arms, his heart, his soul, dictating his destiny. He stared at the sword, wishing he could slice through them all. Cut his way through to freedom.

As Yojiro left the Fortuitous Wind, he knew Takao was watching. Like Obo, he could feel eyes from the shadows.

# Chapter Seven

As Yojiro returned to Shosuro Palace, the night heat cooled. The Hour of the Rat waned into the Hour of the Ox, and the moon sank over the jagged skyline. He slunk along the night-stained gardens and terraces of the Noble Quarter, bruised and somewhat ashamed about his visit to the Fortuitous Wind. He had lost the contents of Obo's desk except for a single letter. The discoveries he did make, such as Aoi and Takao's relationship with Obo, had only revealed more questions than answers. Why would a Kitsuki investigator come to Ryokō Owari with the intention of finding shinobi, become beset with hallucinatory while looking, make allies with a yoriki of the Emerald Magistrate, and then lie to her and his superiors? What was Obo's purpose? And why did he have pupils? What could he possibly have been teaching them?

Takao's kagenari disturbed him most. Yojiro had never seen sorcery such as this before, which seemed to avoid the use of kami altogether. It was similar to what he had heard the most powerful users of Void were cable of, but Takao was clearly no Ishiken of the Phoenix Clan. Where did he learn to use it? Was he shinobi? He was clearly trained for assassination techniques. If he was, for whom? Scorpion? Dragon? Someone else? The excursion had merely multiplied Obo's secrets, and his death hid them all.

The questions rattled inside his mind as Yojiro approached the main gate, which was, oddly, still open. The sound of footfalls echoed just inside the outer walls, so he hid himself in the warped shadow of a nearby white-lilac tree.

*Shadows work both ways.*

About a dozen Thunder Guard with spears emerged, Captain Denmaru leading the way, his marred face scowling in the sinking moonlight. The Thunder Guard captain and his soldiers uniformly marched out into the street and waited. Denmaru sniffed the night air, as if testing the wind. Yojiro held his breath, realizing the stink of the Fishers' Quarter gutter probably still marred his sandals. He pressed himself deeper into the lilac's trunk, praying the tree's perfume could mask his location. Denmaru continued to survey the night a moment longer before more footsteps sounded, coming toward the palace. The governor appeared, sitting in a hanging, open-air sedan chair borne by two servants, accompanied by her own contingent from the Thunder Guard. She nodded to Denmaru as they approached.

"He was at the Theater of Summer Flowers tonight, at a performance of *The Floating World*," she said, her honeyed voice bright with amusement. "That Yasuki play was indeed a most rare treat. It is the only refined thing the Crab Clan have ever produced."

"Why was he there?"

"It seems the magistrate and I share the same passion for the theater as an alibi. He brought a whole troop of his dōshin, too. Either he was worried about being attacked by the actors, or he was desperate for company."

"Or he is making an arrest," Denmaru offered, his voice low with caution. "Was the Seppun woman with him?"

"You know your mark well," Hyobu crooned. "No, she was not, which is why I think he intends something more…exhilarating. One of his personal projects."

A few Thunder Guard soldier fidgeted on their feet at those words, as if they held grave meaning. They turned to observe Denmaru's reaction. Their captain merely nodded.

"Where is he now?"

"He went to the Scarlet Tent after the performance, but I do not know how long he will stay there," Hyobu replied, tilting her head as if she heard something in the distance. She looked out into the skyline. "Opium eaters are not good witnesses."

"As you say."

"And how is our guest?"

"He went for a midnight stroll."

Hyobu let out a small, surprised laugh. "I wonder if he went to the Licensed Quarter after all, and I just missed him. If he did, then his night promises to be eventful. Hopefully, in the right way. Do be careful, Captain. The fool makes for an easy pawn, but you know he has his dangerous moments."

The Thunder Guard captain bowed, and he and his contingent sped down the street in the direction Hyobu had just come from. She followed them with her eyes until they turned the corner, headed west. Then she disappeared with her guards into the castle courtyard, the enormous doors of the gate shutting behind them.

Yojiro crept out from his shadow, the urge to follow Denmaru drawing his footsteps back away from the palace.

Had they been talking about Seno? Why did he need an alibi? What did Hyobu mean about the personal project? And witnesses? Motome's words about Thunder Guard interference came to mind. She hadn't had evidence for her accusations, but could this be an opportunity to confirm her suspicions? Hyobu certainly had sent Denmaru to thwart someone...but whom? And why?

Yojiro stripped off his fishy sandal coverings and concealed them beneath some nearby hydrangeas.

It was time to stare into the soul of Governor Hyobu and her Thunder Guard captain.

Despite the late hour, the small ferry boats to Teardrop Island still teemed with crowds of wealthy sailors, samurai, and nobility, as the staff and services of the Licensed Quarter never slept. As Yojiro disembarked at the wharf on the northern tip of the isle, the air around him trembled with music and laughter. The sounds of shamisen, drums, flutes, koto, and singers swelled like restless wind, the pulse of passionate excitement and abandon. Perfumes of a thousand flowers, oil lamps, and bodies mixed with the invisible, earthy miasma of opium. In front of every tavern, teahouse, gambling parlor, theater, and geisha house, each one painted with the brightest hues, stood sumptuously dressed attendants, beckoning and enticing visitors with promised pleasures beyond their doors. Unlike the rest of the city, Teardrop Island was illumined with legions of lanterns, a new canopy of stars that cast no dread shadows but gladdened every corner with light.

Between him and the district, the crowds of visitors bottlenecked on both sides of the enormous Swords Polished Gate, the entrance into the entertainment paradise. Festooned with hundreds of flowers and gold paper banners, the gate was more of an enormous antechamber where several dozen muscled guards checked each guest for weapons. Maiko geisha milled around the arriving guests, cordially inviting the newcomers in after they surrendered their weapons for "polishing" during the stay.

Yojiro traded his swords for a sea-ivory token with a teardrop and a number carved into its surface, and immediately, a geisha apprentice in pink robes and sparkling silver hair ornaments scattered across her ebony wig singled him out. She gently took his elbow and led him through the gate with dainty steps.

"Good evening, sir," she whispered, sliding back one fold of his raised collar with a poised finger so her gentle, coaxing voice could reach his ear. Her breath tickled his face. "My name is Heaven's Lily, and it is my joy and honor to be your guide during your visit tonight."

"Do I look that lost?" he asked, feigning the charisma of a wealthy pleasure seeker. Inside, he almost recoiled from her attention.

*How convenient. A personal spy for every patron.*

"No one is lost here," she chuckled, her crimson lips curled like loops of silk ribbon around her pearly teeth. "On Teardrop Island, you belong everywhere. Where do you see yourself tonight, samurai-sama? The theater? A teahouse? A private moonlit garden?"

Yojiro shook his head, raising his hand in protest. "No, I am actually looking for someone. An acquaintance."

She smiled sweetly, but her jaw stiffened at his words. "Well, we can certainly look for them. Tell me what they like, and I will surely know where they might be."

"Yes, thank you, Heaven's Lily," Yojiro said, slipping some money into her hands. "But I do not think I will need your guidance tonight."

Her shoulders drooped slightly. "Are you sure? There are plenty of lovely places that I could show you tonight."

"That will not be necessary," he insisted. "I will find my own way."

The apprentice geisha bowed respectfully and deposited the coins into her purse before wandering back through the throngs of the Swords Polished Gate for a new visitor.

Yojiro waded through the rivers of people into the heart of the island. He cut through the mazelike lushness of the Island Garden, strolling past a pair of lovers sharing the cool air beneath blooming wisteria arbors. He skirted a carousing group of young Lion Clan samurai who tumbled out of a sake house and avoided a cloud of singers thronging around a Tortoise Clan samurai who sang refrains of epic poems with them as he passed out coins. Though Yojiro wandered in and around and between the licensed establishments, he did not see even a glimpse of Seno or Denmaru.

As he withdrew from peeking inside a fortune teller's shop, a squat, one-story building, covered in red silk banners to mimic a Unicorn nomadic cloth hut, caught his eye.

*The Scarlet Tent?*

Yojiro approached, and just as he grasped the shōji screen, the door silently slid open a crack. Tendrils of opium-laced steam wafted out into the cool night air. Red light gleamed ominously from the gap, and the melancholy strum of the *biwa* echoed from within.

He cautiously opened the door to the opium den wider, revealing a small, low-ceilinged, blossom-garlanded room aglow in red lantern light. Several steaming water pipes glimmered like black towers on the floor, surrounded by lavish couches and cushions strewn with opulently dressed bodies. A few moved their heads to look at Yojiro, but they immediately shut their eyes, their thoughts lilting away on the rivers of rapture pulsing in their blood. Only the musician, a slender boy with delicate wrists and meticulous fingers, acknowledged his entrance.

"Welcome," he said, strumming his hypnotic rhythm. "Come and indulge."

Yojiro edged back out the door. None of the bodies were Seno or Denmaru, nor did the building have any other exit to suggest separate rooms or back doors.

An icy apprehension nipped the inside of his stomach.

*Was this is a trap? Did Hyobu merely fool me into coming here?*

Yojiro leaned his back against the wall of the opium den, scanning each nearby shadow, door, and shrubbery for surprises. Ragged moments passed, and eventually, his heart eased back down to its normal gait.

"Strange night," came a weak voice from inside the Scarlet Tent. A man with long, silvery hair and a blue fan absently swished fireflies away from the door as he emerged. He opened a tiny porcelain case and smeared a tiny glob of poppy tar onto his finger, which he subsequently rolled into a ball between his finger and thumb. He then stuck the pill to the roof of his mouth and sighed. "The Thunder Guard did the same thing you did. Took one look and vanished."

*Was this part of the trap?*

He felt the visceral panic of helplessness without his swords at his side. He balled his fists.

"You saw the Thunder Guard?" Yojiro asked, careful to keep his eyes on his surroundings. "Where did they go?"

"They went that way, toward that glow of sunrise," the opium eater mumbled, pointing to the sky where an orange spark shone above the rooftop of another nearby geisha house.

"That is not east," Yojiro mumbled, staring as the orange stain in the black sky.

*Fire?*

He wandered toward the direction of the flames. They were still small yet, barely larger than Hyobu's sedan chair. Manageable, but no one had seen them yet.

Suddenly, an elderly gentleman slammed into him, knocking both of them onto the street. The bruises from his fight with Takao screamed in pain at the new agitation, but he leaped to his feet, offering his hand to the poor man.

"Please forgive me, sir!" Yojiro babbled, pulling the man from the ground and proceeding to dust the man's silk clothes. There were singe marks all over him. Then, the Otomo crest with the magisterial green orb stopped him dead. It was Otomo Seno.

"Scorpion!" Seno barked, his face livid as he straightened his hat. "How dare you? First, I see that skulking, stalking Thunder Guard captain, and now I run into you! The two of you are in league! Both of you! Conspirators!"

Yojiro took a step back. "Forgive me, Otomo-sama, I meant no offense. I was merely in a hurry to help—"

"Arrest him!" Seno yelled, throwing his hands in the air. Seno's half-dozen dōshin eyed each other warily, but they shuffled forward. "Ninja conspirator!"

"But look at the fire," Yojiro contended, his voice rising. He pointed in the direction of the flames.

The roof lay dark.

At first, Yojiro stared, his eyes wide in incredulous panic, but he realized that someone must have already extinguished the flames. The telling, lingering smell of the fire still hung thick in the air, right in front of him.

"You helped start the fire, you say?" Seno asked, his furious red face turning even more scarlet. His frustrated anger suddenly melted into the sneering belligerence of victory. "I knew there was something evil about you, Bayushi. Arrest him!"

The dōshin grasped his arms tightly and marched him toward the Swords Polished Gate. A sizeable crowd of curious onlookers stared at them. In the sea of faces, Yojiro spotted Denmaru and his Thunder Guard. They locked eyes for one moment, the gruff Shosuro captain's face twisted in slight amusement. He turned his back and walked away.

# Chapter Eight

Day dawned mere hours later in Ryokō Owari Prison, but the sun made no difference in the light of Seno's blinding lamps to ward against ninja. Yojiro had sat on his heels those few hours in his cell, a squat filthy cage strewn with hay. It was not tall enough to stand in, but he didn't dare sit in the grime or let his guard down.

He shared company with the Storm Tigers, though the ruffians scarcely moved, even as dawn rose. Their bodies were broken and bleeding from their interrogation the day before, the one that had convicted them as ninja. Several Storm Tigers had mangled hands or feet, while others had sustained a variety of flesh wounds and burn marks. Buyu, the pitiful rickshaw puller, had fewer marks, probably having given up his confession easily.

Yojiro could not banish the memory of Denmaru's smile. The gloat of a trap well sprung? Yet, the events had only developed as a random set of accidents. Yojiro's detour to Teardrop Island. Running into Seno. Seno arresting him out of anger. Denmaru's appearance right at the end.

Conspirators, Seno had called them. Ninja conspirators.

Could Hyobu and Denmaru have orchestrated it all?

As if conjured from the air, the cell block doors opened, and the

Thunder Guard captain entered, a few infantry in tow, carrying spears.

"Good morning, Yojiro-sama," he said disinterestedly, motioning for one of Seno's dōshin to unlock the cell. The guard was hesitant until Denmaru flashed an edict signed by Hyobu in his face. Yojiro's swords hung from his obi beside his own. "Governor Hyobu has heard of your arrest and has judged, upon review of the events last night, that according to her laws, your arrest was a mere magisterial misunderstanding. You are free to go."

"Wait, Captain Denmaru," Yojiro stepped over Buyu's still-snoring form and out of the cell. He bowed once in forced thanks and took his swords back, but propriety could not overcome his scowl as they met eye to eye. The night had drained his patient etiquette. "What happened last night?"

Denmaru's eyes narrowed in annoyance at Yojiro's question. "A magisterial misunderstanding."

"But what you were you doing there last night?" Yojiro nearly demanded, his endurance wearing thin. "The fire? The arrest? What did you do to Otomo-sama that made him lash out at me? What were you and Governor Hyobu plotting?"

The captain's eyes grew stonier than his skin. His jaw tightened, and he nearly raised a scarred hand as if to strike Yojiro, but one of his soldiers grunted and he lowered it. "You should know better than to accuse a fellow Scorpion. You sound more and more like that fool Otomo."

"Then tell me, Captain."

"If you are looking for shadows, you will find them," he hissed. "And you may just burn your whole world down trying to get rid of them."

Frustration gnawed at Yojiro as he approached Motome's office in the vault. He wished he could erase the night before. One Scorpion Clan secret had sprouted after another, choking him with their dishonor like foul weeds. Shinobi. Sabotage. Hedonism. Murder.

Luckily, his high collar concealed the deep-purple welt on his jawline from his tumble down the stairs at the Fortuitous Wind, so Motome wouldn't know how much it battered him, inside and out.

"You did not sleep," Motome observed, looking up only briefly from her work on a map of Ryokō Owari Toshi spread out over her desk. She busily marked it with red ink, occasionally referencing

Obo's geisha-house log. Sticking silver needles into the wood of the walls, she had pinned up all of Obo's desk documents they had gathered the day before, grouping and fanning them out by content. She had also pinned all of her tiny slip messages from Obo near them, creating a woven timeline of papers.

She must have spent all night doing it. And she was concerned that *he* hadn't slept.

"Did you go out last night?" she asked, pausing in her work a moment to stare at him. The warmth in her eyes revealed more interest than suspicion.

Yojiro was in no mood for lies this morning. "Yes."

"And?"

"I learned Ryokō Owari is dangerous at night."

Motome only just stifled a laugh. "Yes. It is. You were robbed, weren't you?"

Yojiro smirked, her bluntness putting him at ease. Honesty was indeed a simpler way to live. "After a fashion. That was the second time in two days."

"What?" Her eyes grew wide and round.

He grimaced, embarrassed at her incredulous tone. Maybe he was being too honest.

"Perhaps the Fortune of Wealth is displeased with you, Yojiro-sama. You should visit his temple and make an offering to appease him. I can show you the way if you would like."

Yojiro flushed. No one had ever offered to accompany him on a private outing. Not even Mikuru, who had been too busy living her own life, following her own duties. He wasn't sure how to respond. Decorum dictated that he decline, at least once, for humility's sake. But he did want to go with her. How did one respond beyond the polite, detached refusal?

"I would be grateful, Motome-san, if your offer was in earnest."

"Of course. We have reason to go to the Temple Quarter anyway."

"Oh?" Yojiro cocked his head in surprise.

She pointed to Obo's slips pinned to the wall. "I organized them, as you suggested, and I found a pattern. The log mentions locations scattered all over Ryokō Owari, but Kitsuki-sama mentions the Temple of Amaterasu the most, in the greatest detail."

Yojiro shook his head. Obo had been lying to Motome, just like he had been lying to his superiors at the Kitsuki School of Investigation. "I am not sure that you can trust those slips, Motome-san."

"No, listen to me," Motome growled, knitting her eyebrows in frustration. "I know you still do not believe that there are shinobi. You believe that Kitsuki-sama was fanatical, driven by fear, perhaps like Otomo-sama. But this is important."

Yojiro, cowed by her anger, lowered his eyes. "Forgive me. Please go on."

Motome puckered her mouth in sour satisfaction. She pointed to the slips she had marked in red ink. "Kitsuki-sama's messages about the Temple of Amaterasu all occur on the first day of the month."

Yojiro's jaw dropped open. "What?"

She pointed to the wall, indicating one slip that mentioned the temple.

"Gathering planned. Rooftop of Temple of Amaterasu. Date undetermined. Will observe the area."

She lifted the slip, exposing the other side.

"The Month of the Ox, first day."

"He did not send them to me consistently, but whenever he mentioned that temple, the message arrived on the first day of a new month, and those arrived almost every month." She pointed and flipped through the ten years' worth of red-marked slips.

"Northern garden. Temple of Amaterasu. Two figures congregating near the okame cherry trees. The Month of the Hare, first day."

"Temple of Amaterasu courtyard. Footprints on the wall. Someone tried to climb the roof. First day of the Month of the Rooster."

"But why that day?" Yojiro asked, his mind picking apart the weeks and days of their lunar calendar to find some inkling of Obo's obsession with the Temple of Amaterasu. Perhaps Obo merely developed a cyclical system to trick her, to vary his lies over the months.

"I am not sure," she said, picking up Obo's pleasure-house ledger. "But look at this." Opening the book to a page she had marked in red ink and pointing, she revealed the same pattern. On the same days of the month, there were entries of:

"Month of the Ox, first day. House of the Plum Blossom. Funa."

"Month of the Hare, first day. House of the Crashing Wave. Nobu."

"Month of the Rooster, first day. House of the Morning Star. Aoi."

*Aoi? It can't be.*

Yojiro tore the ledger from Motome's grasp and scoured the names she had circled in red. Names of all genders. Each associated with a pleasure house. Each date coinciding with a date on one of Obo's messages to Motome, as if he had attended the pleasure house the same day he reported going to the Temple of Amaterasu.

The date next to Aoi's name was only just over a year ago. Had she worked in a geisha house until just recently? Perhaps it was not the same person. However, none of the names in the log repeated. Could Obo know two people named Aoi, both a geisha and his student?

Being so fixated on Denmaru, he had not thought to ask the geisha proprietors on Teardrop Island about these names.

"I am sure that we will find something to tie all of these together if we go to the Temple Quarter," Motome said, folding her arms and leaning back on her zabuton. Her excitement made her body tremble, though her cheeks were drooped slightly from exhaustion.

Yojiro shook his head in disbelief, smiling. "Motome-san. You are an exceptional investigator."

She shook her hand. "No, no, you flatter me, Yojiro-sama," she laughed, modestly. She stood to tuck her swords and jitte into her obi. "I am merely stubborn. I wanted you to believe in Kitsuki-sama's shinobi story so much that I stayed awake all night, obsessing. Perhaps I am learning well under Otomo-sama's example."

Yojiro opened the door for her, not sure if he should smile at the irony of her words or grimace after last night. "I think he would do well to learn from yours."

The golden Temple Quarter lay east of the Merchant Quarter, a true opposite side of the coin. While the markets were a maze of dark alleys, this district dedicated to the gods was bathed in sunlight. Wide streets flowed between tranquil meditation parks filled with glassy lotus ponds and raked stone gardens.

Studding the roads were peaked shrines and temples devoted to the Ten Thousand Fortunes. Some sanctuaries, tiny as paper fans, housed collections of stone statues of the kami dressed in silk shawls and woven grass talismans for good luck. Larger temples and shrines dedicated to the Seven Fortunes contained enormous bronze or gold statues and boasted their own worship halls filled with whole congregations of reverent followers.

Towering above them all, however, was the immense, thirteen-tiered shining pagoda of Daikoku-no-Kami, whose shadow was said to bless all it touched. The Temple of Daikoku retained nearly one hundred monks, whose daily chanting and prayers rang in the air, blending with the sandalwood and aloe incense smoke that fluttered throughout the quarter.

Yojiro and Motome had only just entered the district, passing a courtyard fountain where novice priests sat in contemplation, when Yojiro spotted Ikku's red palanquin. Instead of lurking in the shadows, the crimson silk carriage boldly passed by on the arms of its bearers. Hovering in the distance, it continued behind an enormous bronze bell hung from a grey cypress belfry, headed in the direction of the Temple of Daikoku.

*What could he be doing here?*

"Did you hear me, Yojiro-sama?" Motome asked, pointing the opposite way. "The Temple of Amaterasu is down this street."

"Excuse me. I thought I saw someone I recognized," Yojiro apologized. The palanquin was gone. "Please, lead the way."

As they rounded the corner of an incense shop, a sharp light burned Yojiro's eyes. His hand shot up to shield himself. High above his head, at the height of an enormous camphor tree, hung a dazzling spherical mirror crowned with a golden ring of fiery rays. The mirror rested on a thick brass minaret in the center of the temple's shimmering limestone courtyard, with seven sacred buildings gathered about it. Motome led the way to the smallest of the buildings, drawing another search warrant from her sleeve. She had done much more work than he had realized.

"Excuse me, venerable sir," she said, approaching and bowing to a shugenja garbed in robes of intense saffron. He wore a straw, mushroomlike hat upon his head, which shielded his eyes from his surroundings, and he plied garnet prayer beads with calm, methodical fingers. "We come from the Emerald Magistrate to investigate particular circumstances surrounding a deceased Dragon Clan minister. His name was Kitsuki Obo, and we have reason to believe he might have come here often."

"Everyone comes here," the priest answered, an aloof smokiness to his voice. He did not look at them, merely staring into the shade of his hat, avoiding the distractions of the physical world. "This is the temple where we honor Lady Sun's light. The mother of the Kami blesses all, and they in turn come to thank her."

Motome nodded, more out of delicacy than sincerity. "Of course. We have come to inquire after one of her worshippers, someone who came monthly, perhaps."

"Her light blinds. Her light heals," the priest continued, his voice taking on the reverent intonations of a chant. "And so, all come to worship her, to see what she reveals in them."

Motome looked at Yojiro, unsure of what to do. He shrugged. If the priest was lost in the loop of his liturgy, this could take time. Finally, she waved him on, indicating that she would speak to the priest while Yojiro searched the rest of the complex. He nodded, slowly backing away from the conversation to avoid offending the priest.

He wandered toward the nearest of the seven shrines: a two-story, white-walled sacred hall with a black roof forked with spires along the top. White-pine plaques marked the building as having been dedicated in honor of both Amaterasu and Onnotangu, Sun and Moon, mother and father to the Kami.

As he entered the sanctuary, taking off his shoes, he saw in lieu of a statue an enormous mural carved into golden *kiri* wood. The masterful relief mimicked the sky, with swirls and stars. Inlaid across its surface, round glass mirrors representing Amaterasu chased intricately carved ivory disks representing Onnotangu. Lord Moon waxed and waned in its phases, its black side covered in a roughly hewn ebony.

The relief told the story of the Moon, the fickle lover whose passions cooled in jealousy over Lady Sun's love for their children. Eventually, the envious Moon grew completely black, extinguishing his love for her, which marked the day he betrayed Amaterasu and swallowed their Kami children. The complete ebony disk, the night with no light, marked when Amaterasu wept for her children.

Yojiro stared at this last disk. The blackest night. Despite the despair of the black moon, from this night emerged hope, as Amaterasu had saved her final child—the Kami Hantei, blessed ancestor of the Emperor's family—from being swallowed in order to save his siblings. The Rokugani marked the black moon as the start of their lunar calendar in deference to Hantei, the Blessed Son of

Heaven, who saved the Kami and grew to rule Rokugan. The first day of every new month.

As he studied the artistically rough edges of the final ebony disk, a flaw emerged. There, in the center of the disk, concealed in the black eddies of the carving, was a secret switch no larger than the tip of his little finger.

Yojiro swallowed. *Scorpion craftsmanship, again.*

But he was sharing the shrine with an old shugenja who lay prostrate, praying to the Kami, her forehead touching the smooth elm floor. She muttered her swift, complex prayers, barely pausing for breath. Yojiro cleared his throat, but she did not move, absorbed in deep communion with her deities.

*Perhaps she will not notice.*

He drew his coin pouch out of his pocket, twisted a corner into a dense knot, and gently pressed the button, hoping the Scorpion craftsperson had oiled the mechanisms. No needle shot out this time, but Yojiro could hear the faint spin of a pulley.

A panel the size of a cartwheel slid open in the wall to Yojiro's right, silent as a breath. He froze.

The shugenja's prayers droned on, undisturbed. Yojiro slipped into the opening moments before it shut, enveloping him in darkness.

He waited for several minutes, pressing his ear against the panel door, listening for any reaction from the shugenja, but he heard nothing. The ashen smell of dust and spider silk tickled his nose. There was no fleck of sunlight in this strange, walled passage, so his eyes could not adjust.

He had not thought to bring his candle and fire striker on the daytime outing, so he cautiously spread his hands out to feel. The passage, about as narrow as the length of his katana, was walled with splintering wood that gouged and pricked at his skin. He stumbled upon a raised plank in front of him, the first step of a steep staircase leading up toward the back of the shrine, behind the relief. Warily, he crawled up the steps, keeping his hands before and above him. The stairs groaned beneath him ever so slightly, like the grim, faint moan of the dying.

A sharp, searing pain raked one of his hands, so he snatched it back. Feeling his flesh in the dark, he perceived that a fine cut had opened across his palm. He traced the pain in a straight line.

*Razor thread.*

Drawing his wakizashi, he sliced the air in front of him, hearing the *ping* as the wire snapped against his blade. He continued up, his short sword now before him.

Finally, after he had crawled the height of the shrine, his weapon collided into another door. Finding the handle, he cautiously slid it open. Grey streams of light filtered in from a few fist-sized air vents in the far wall, illuminating a small room with a sloped ceiling. He figured he was in a tiny space between the vast relief and the back wall, just behind the eaves of the shrine. A few brass oil lamps dangled, hovering over what appeared to be a red-pine workbench scattered with tools. Yojiro lit one with a nearby steel fire striker. His stomach pitched.

Beneath a scattering of long iron needles, clay pots of oozing black paste, and sets of shackles, the surface of the workbench was spattered with dried blood. Years of stains had pooled into the wood, warping its surface slightly, crusting into a cruel, blackish veneer.

Ignoring his stomach, he studied the instruments without touching them. They looked like tattoo lances, meaning the pots were full of foul-smelling pigments. The chains were on the slimmer side, meant to hold secure the wrists and ankles of a young person, though not quite small enough for a child.

On the wall above the workbench hung a leather diagram of the human body, front and back, with strange symbols etched all over the skin. They looked just like the marks on Takao's arm, a secret language scrawled in serpentine crescents. Next to the grim drawing hung a scrap of kimono, upon which was embroidered the Scorpion crest.

*Obo, what did you discover here?*

Yojiro's throat tightened as his heart trembled in his chest. This was the secret that drove Obo to the brink with fear ten years ago. The secret the Scorpion would kill to keep hidden. This was why Obo had begged Motome for help, for protection. This was what Aramoro knew and wouldn't say.

*How could the Scorpion hide such depraved rituals? How could Aramoro, Kachiko even, defile the purity of their station with these wicked secrets?*

He needed to confront Aramoro and get the answers. Now. Ignoring his writhing stomach, Yojiro ripped the diagram and the silk crest from the wall, rolled them up, and thrust them into his breast pocket. He blew out the lamp and stumbled quietly back down the stairs, white-hot anger beginning to boil in his chest.

He cursed Kachiko for threatening him. He cursed her for condemning his honor. He clenched his fingers so tight it nearly snapped his knuckles.

*She will answer for this. So will Aramoro. I will tell Motome. I will tell Toturi. I will tell the Emperor that there is rotting flesh in the depths of my clan. I will expose it to be burned with the light of the sun, cleansed from this world.*

Yojiro spread his fingers wide to search for a latch to open the panel in the wall. It was tucked into the side. Yojiro pressed it, again using his coin pouch. The panel slid open, blinding him for a moment with the sun. He blinked. The shrine was empty. Even the praying shugenja was gone. But he no longer cared who saw. The truth needed to be revealed.

He strode out into the sunlight, searching for Motome. He rushed around the other shrines, weaving in between priests and worshipping visitors. Several of them gave him flustered glares as he shoved past them to look into a building only to hurry out again, but he ignored it. He needed to tell her. His heart galloped.

She was not in the temple. Frantic, he darted out of the compound's gate into the street. Though several dozen reverent pedestrians bustled in both directions along the road, Motome's tiny figure was not among them.

*Maybe she returned to the reformatory.*

He scurried down the street in the direction of the Merchant Quarter. Its dark alleys loomed ahead. He plunged into one, only to nearly crash into the front door of a pickle shop. The store's sign clattered as he barely nudged it before halting. A dead end.

Not waiting for his eyes to adjust, he backed up and tried another. He rounded the corner, nearly running now.

Suddenly, he slammed into a hulking figure. He cracked his head against its shoulder and nearly tumbled to the ground. Grunting, he clutched his bruised skull in both hands.

"Please forgive me," he stammered, his cheeks flushed with

panicked shame. "I did not see you."

As the stars left his eyes, his shoulders tensed. His hand flashed to his katana. He had crashed into the muscular arm of a man bearing a red silk palanquin on the opposite shoulder. The brute snarled and cursed under his breath.

"What is it?" that cruel, hissing voice called from behind the crimson curtain. It lifted, revealing the ratty face of Ikku.

# Chapter Nine

"Ah, Magistrate," Ikku chuckled as his servants lowered his palanquin to the ground. He stepped out, whirling his scorpion pipe in eager fingers. "It is pleasant to see you again so soon. You just caught me on my way back from my morning prayer to Daikoku-no-Kami for today's fortune. It seems he feels particularly generous today."

"I do not have time to meddle with you, Ikku," Yojiro grumbled. His hand clenched around the silken ties of his katana hilt.

Ikku's bellowing laugh filled the close confines of the alley, reverberating in the overbearing eaves. "Time can be bought, Magistrate. Your choice, as always."

Yojiro's thumb raised his katana a degree, threatening Ikku, but the crime lord merely gestured to his minions. Ikku's six gangsters snatched thick mountain-ash *tetsubō* hidden beneath the palanquin. Swinging the slender clubs bound with iron rings, they moved to encircle Yojiro. The samurai drew his sword fully, hoping his steel would deter them.

"I will cut through each one of you if I have to," he warned, crouching into a striking stance.

"My loyal servants have toppled your kind before, Magistrate," the crime lord said indifferently. "Get him."

The gangsters hurled themselves at Yojiro, careful from experience to coordinate their swings in the narrow space. Yojiro ducked under the arm of one to escape the circle, but they all swung around, shifting their formation to catch him in another ring against the opposite alley wall. One criminal swung at Yojiro's side, and as he moved to dodge, a second tough aimed high, ready to strike Yojiro's head as it came within reach. Yojiro dropped beneath the swing and sprang up on its back side, slashing clean through the headhunter's wrists on the way up, but a third brute had already caught Yojiro in the thigh with his tetsubō. Luckily, the end of the club hit the wall, dispersing the force, but Yojiro's knee still buckled in pain, and he fell, that side of his body crumpling into the ground.

*Keep moving. You need to clutter their timing!*

Continuing the motion from his fall, Yojiro tumbled out from under a hail of blows. The end of the alley loomed dangerously nearer as the gangsters drove him toward the corner. He leaped forward, taking the offensive, slashing in a wide arc to gain ground. One brute lunged, wildly smashing her cudgel down on top of Yojiro's katana, forcing his cut down into the cobblestones. The steel rang against the stone, and the shudder vibrated up his arms into his shoulders.

*They are trying to break my sword! I need to end this!*

He reclaimed his momentum, slashing down into the gangster's unprotected neck. Slicing through the bone, however, Yojiro's blade stuck. He jumped, wrenching it free with the counterweight of his whole body, but the delay mistimed a necessary dodge as a fifth criminal's club, aimed high, crunched into the side of his head.

He couldn't see. A metallic ringing swirled inside his skull, and he collapsed on the street, his katana slipping from his limp fingers. Time slowed as muffled cries rent the air, preceding the final blows. He could only wait. The street was cold.

No new blows fell. Someone was lifting him, shaking him in the dark.

"Yojiro!"

It was Motome.

"Yojiro! Wake up!" He opened his eyes. He could only see her mouth. "Yojiro, you need to breathe."

She tried to lift him, but he slipped out of her arms, doubling over in the street. As he hunched over on the cobblestones, nausea swept over him, shuddering in his spine and through his belly. After a few moments, Yojiro breathlessly nodded his thanks to her, the searing pounding of his lungs still refusing to abate. He eased down, leaning back against the wall, the cool wood steadying his head. Slowly, his breath returned, and it merged into a laugh, relief gradually releasing the rigidity of his body.

"Motome-san," he wheezed, mirth painting his voice. "Thank you."

"Are you okay? Just moments ago, you looked dead."

He tried to nod, but the resounding pain in his head cut him short.

"Give me a few more moments to collect myself," Yojiro replied.

"I'm so sorry I left you. When I finished with the priest, I could not find you, so I thought you had gone to the Temple of Daikoku without me."

Yojiro smiled weakly. "And I thought you had headed back to the reformatory, so we went opposite ways."

As his sight refocused, a body came into view. And another. Motome sat back on her heels, jitte firmly in hand, its forked prong streaked with blood. All around her lay the gangsters, unconscious or dead, some with broken wrists and fingers, a few missing teeth—or, in one case, hands. Ikku too lay a little distance off, limp and crumpled in a heap like a cast-off garment.

Motome, still somewhat winded from her own skirmish, laughed, relief relaxing her face from her intensely concentrated battle scowl. "We did not leave an offering at the Temple of Daikoku, Yojiro-sama," she said. "Your bad fortune is still following you."

Yojiro pulled his purse from his kimono and tossed it onto the heap of defeated rogues. "Our offering," he wheezed, "to Daikoku-no-Kami. He can have the whole pile."

Motome smiled and cleaned her jitte on a handkerchief before sliding it back into her obi. "I think he will be pleased. How does your head feel?"

Yojiro caressed the dull lump forming behind his ear. An ache beat deep within it. "Nothing debilitating."

"As long as you can walk." She helped him to his feet. Her warm eyes grew grave, wilting her smile somewhat. "I have bad news, Yojiro-sama."

Her sorrow sharpened his focus. "Oh?"

Then he remembered his own bad news. His wicked discovery in the garret in the Shrine of Onnotangu. His chest clenched.

"Not here," she said, steadying Yojiro's gait with a hand at his elbow. She gestured toward the shadows. "In private."

He nodded. The secret chafed inside his soul. Seething. Rioting. It bound him up, the Scorpion shame tangling around him in thick cords, suffocating him.

*I will tell her everything. I will expose the rot. Then I can be free.*

They shuffled down the street toward the reformatory, Yojiro leaning on Motome's strength.

"What?"

Yojiro's jaw dropped. He pressed his fingers into his eyes, the answers in his head splitting into a hundred new pieces, renewing the whirl of confusion. He drooped beneath the weight of them, the clashing possibilities taking the floor out from underneath him.

"You were right to be suspicious of him," Motome nearly wailed, her voice weak and bitter with regret. She slumped down upon a zabuton in her office, clutching at the silk cushion with sorrow-clenched hands. "Kitsuki Obo was a child stealer. The priest at the Temple of Amaterasu said as much. Those awful rumors I heard in the North Rim were true. I was such a fool to trust him!"

*"Dazzled by hope's bright star,"* Obo had written about her in his journal. He had deceived her from the first day.

"What did the priest tell you?" Yojiro asked, pacing around the room, the knot on his head throbbing, nearly urging him into a frenzy.

"He remembered the Kitsuki visiting the temple every few months, always on the first day of the month as we suspected, the day of the black moon, just as the sun was setting. He made offerings in the Shrine of Onnotangu, and he would always be accompanied by a teenaged street orphan from the Fishers' Quarter. The priest always knew because they smelled so strongly. The Kitsuki would come with a different youth each time."

Yojiro cringed.

*A different youth. Every few months. For ten years.*

Gruesome images wavered in his mind. The needles. Shackles. The workbench awash in blood.

He gritted his teeth. "Did the priest know why the Kitsuki

brought them there?"

"No," she mumbled, "but he always pointed to the relief while whispering at length. The priest thought maybe he was teaching the orphans the story of the Kami, but when none of them ever returned, he simply judged the man to be a poor missionary."

Yojiro recalled the diagram he had taken from the wall in that wretched place. The pattern dictating which serpentine symbols Obo undoubtedly chiseled into the youths' flesh.

*Takao...Takao had one branded upon his arm.*

Yojiro snatched the pleasure-house ledger from Motome's desk and thumbed through the earlier entries, skimming each name she had marked as those coinciding with the first day of the month. He passed Aoi's name near the front. Several dozen new-moon names into the register, he found it.

"Month of the Tiger, first day. House of Foreign Stories. Takao."

Yojiro nearly dropped the book. The ledger was not a list of Obo's encounters at pleasure houses. This was a coded archive of his rituals. He had recorded the names of his victims.

Both Takao and Aoi had gone through this ritual, tortured at Obo's hand. Yet they called him "sensei." They were his pupils, students who mourned his loss. Takao had even threatened to kill Yojiro for coming too close to their secret. A secret he would kill to protect...Was this ritual their secret? What had Obo done to them?

Yojiro flipped through the names once more. Takao. House of Foreign Stories. Aoi. House of the Morning Star. The geisha-house names varied, barely a half dozen matching Takao's house and many more coming from the House of the Plum Blossom. Perhaps they expressed a code...some encrypted description of the outcomes of the ritual? Aoi had said that there had been other pupils, but that they had abandoned the school after Obo was killed.

"What is it?" Motome asked, interrupting his thoughts. She had already started taking down Obo's slips of paper from the wall, her fingers listless with regret, shoving them into their maple-wood box. "Have you found more damaging evidence against his character?"

Yojiro tried to ignore her as his mind raced through the events, straining to connect them.

*A Kitsuki investigator is sent to Ryokō Owari to find shinobi. He becomes delusional while looking. He recruits one of the Emerald*

*Magistrate's yoriki. He lies to her and his superiors, feeding them false information. And yet, he gives Seppun Motome secret clues to his wicked vice, kidnapping youths to torture. However, those tortured become his pupils. He is then murdered...by the Scorpion?*

His entire body shuddered in confusion. He feverishly combed through the chaos of clues that lay piled around them, pinned to the walls, tucked into boxes, thrown in baskets.

*The pieces will not come together. They simply do not fit.*

Yojiro spied the basket of Obo's bloody clothes. The clothes that had been too wide. Taken from someone else. Retailored to fit.

The truth settled down on him, like a frozen mist, chilling his heart.

*I need proof.*

He snatched the jade dragon ring and stuck it on, then tried it on different fingers in a wild juggle. Inside the rim of the ring, a piece of green-stained wax had refitted it to accommodate a smaller finger. Yojiro discreetly ripped the wax away. The ring now sagged enormously, even around his thumb, an ornament meant for broad, stocky fingers.

Yojiro seized the porcelain urn of Obo's ashes and broke the sticky prayer seal. A dusky scent eased out of the jar. Muttering an apology to the deceased, he snatched up Motome's writing brush and stirred about inside the urn for any bone fragments, careful not to touch the defiling pieces of the dead. A few charred bits rose to the top. Finally, what he was looking for breached the surface of the ash. One finger bone. It was delicate, from a finger even thinner than his own, a finger from a hand too small to wear this ring without the wax.

"Yojiro-sama?" Motome stared up at him, her mouth and cheeks trembling with dread as he fished the bones out with chopsticks and folded them up in a scrap of paper. "What are you doing?"

"I need to speak with Aramoro," Yojiro said, slipping the bones and ring into his pocket and mashing the wax seal shoddily back into place on the urn. "Now."

"What is this about?"

Yojiro merely stared straight into her light eyes. They were wide, warm, but somewhat fearful. "Trust me."

# Chapter Ten

Aramoro was in the reformatory's gravel courtyard, taking a guarded stroll for air and sunlight, three dōshin escorting him from behind, keeping an obviously intimidated distance from "the Whisper of Steel" and his cruel tongue.

"What have you come to see me about, lapdog?" Aramoro growled, disgust still contorting his wild, unshaven face. "Have you come to beg?"

Yojiro eyed the guards, who might still be in earshot.

"Shall we sit? Perhaps at the edge of that waterfall?" he suggested, pointing to Seno's eavesdropper guard. Aramoro smirked. The water crashed across the stones, frothing in boiling chaos above the principle "Meiyo," muffling their words as they spoke.

"I know that you did not kill Kitsuki Obo," Yojiro said. He drew the finger bones, ring, and green wax from his pocket, showing them to Aramoro in the paper they were wrapped in only for a moment before hiding them again. "This ring is too large for the dead man lying in that urn, yet it is Obo's ring. And the clothes the dead man wore the night you killed him. They had been tailored to fit the man in the urn, altered from the size of a man who would fit this ring."

"Clever observation," Aramoro chuckled. "What does it mean?"

Yojiro drew out his single remaining letter from Obo's desk. "I found this letter from the Kitsuki investigators dated one month ago. They claim not only to have informants in our own spy network, but also to suspect us of using shinobi. They sent Obo to Ryokō Owari twelve years ago expressly with the purpose of finding them. However, in this letter, they warn Obo of a man named Soshi Ezo, a dangerous Scorpion shinobi who was rumored to still be alive after faking his own death ten years ago."

Aramoro's smile grew darker, taunting even. "And did Kitsuki Obo find this Soshi Ezo?"

Yojiro folded his arms, refusing to falter at the trick question. "He did, but not after receiving this letter telling him to find Ezo. He actually found Ezo ten years before the letter. I read an account from his journal that suggests that ten years ago, he discovered a terrible Scorpion secret. Kitsuki Obo found evidence that a group was tattooing their bodies in dark rituals to grant themselves the ability to become one with shadows. This made him delusional, his mind frantic with fear as every shadow appeared to be an enemy. However, his nightmares became reality. He was intercepted and silently replaced soon after by Soshi Ezo. Then Ezo, who adopted Obo's identity, worked to hide what Obo had discovered by lying to the Kitsuki investigators ever since."

"So you suggest that I killed Soshi Ezo and not a Kitsuki investigator like everyone believes? Why would I do that? He sounds quite useful."

"You would only kill someone like that if ordered to. And that order would only come if he were a danger to our clan—if he threatened us in some way. With his 'kagenari,' he must have. This explains why the clan picked you to take care of Ezo. Only the Whisper of Steel could cut down a shadow."

Aramoro rubbed his coarse chin in amusement, his angular teeth flashing in the sun. "Me, take down a shadow master? You flatter me. How do you know Ezo used kagenari?"

"The Kitsuki investigators knew and wrote about it in their letter. Apparently, Ezo was infamous for his skill with it. The investigators called him the most dangerous shinobi our clan has ever produced."

"Still, I don't why you would think such a…magnificent asset would deserve death."

Yojiro swallowed, the complex strands of the story finally weaving together.

"I met two of Ezo's pupils who knew. They refused to tell me why their master was killed, yet unwittingly revealed the reason to me. The young woman was an exceptional illusionist, trained by Ezo to impersonate others quite well. The other pupil, a young man, I saw was marked with the kagenari shadow brand. From what I discovered about the school and its rituals, however, it seems that both must have been given the shadow brand, but only the young man could wield it."

"Interesting. Go on."

"For the students, neither of these abilities were secrets they felt they needed to protect by killing me. This means that our clan was not threatened by these secret arts. No, what these pupils needed to hide was a secret that endangered them personally."

Aramoro clapped, a raw amusement staining his bedraggled face. "And what was that?"

"Ezo did not fake his death strictly to become Obo. Rather, he faked his death to escape from the Scorpion. To avoid punishment. An execution, even. I think his habit of forcefully branding his students might explain it. After faking his death, he fled here but secretly longed to return to the Scorpion's good graces. I found this in his workshop." Yojiro withdrew the tattered Scorpion crest Ezo had pinned to the wall next to his kagenari diagram. "He came to a Scorpion city, he destroyed a significant menace to the clan, and he purposefully fed false information to more clan enemies, hoping to regain the Scorpion's good graces. He worked tirelessly for ten years at it before revealing himself and his good work to the clan once more. However, since he had been unable to refrain from his original sin of torturing people, you killed him."

"Clever, Yojiro." Aramoro leered, his smile dangerously calm. He dipped his hand into the fountain, tracing circles upon the water's glassy surface. "You almost have it all right."

"What did I get wrong?" Yojiro paused, reviewing his story. Obo's delusions. Ezo's impersonation. Aoi and Takao.

"Now permit me tell you a story, Yojiro," Aramoro said, his eyes dimming as he delved far into his memories, his fingers plunging deeper into the fountain pool. "Decades ago, Soshi Ezo and I trained at the same fighting schools, learning the same techniques and following the same path. We even learned ninjutsu, mastering all the discreet arts. However, we eventually parted ways when he took the oaths to become an actual shinobi, a path I could not follow, as I was a noble's son. 'You are too conspicuous,' they said.

"However, the real reason, Yojiro, was because my family did not want me to give up Bushidō. You see, shinobi become *hinin*, the lowest of castes. Those who deal in filth and excrement. Those who touch the dead and torture the guilty. Those who relinquish their bodies to others' pleasure. I was too important to become a warrior with no honor, no identity, the lowest status in the Celestial Order. My primary duty was to continue being a Bayushi samurai. But Ezo's was not."

"So the clan has been using dishonorable warriors for that long?"

"What clan hasn't, Yojiro?" Aramoro grunted. "Do not judge the vine for adapting to the shape of the tree it grows on. The Scorpion only ever do as they must. We do not cower from our duty."

Yojiro bit his lip. "So Ezo became shinobi, for the clan."

"Yes," Aramoro continued. "Yet somehow, he relished it. He enjoyed the freedom of a life without Bushidō, without the constraints of the Celestial Order, without needing to adhere to tenets like Righteousness, Sincerity, or Honor. Yet, a shinobi still has their own rules. However, as a dishonored man—despite having been given purpose by a Great Clan—Ezo sunk deeper into his depravity, beginning to ignore the shinobi code, acting less like a loyal retainer and more like a wild demon.

"And just as you say, about ten years ago, Ezo was discovered experimenting with kagenari, more dishonorable than poison, crossing a new line of corruption. His tests killed many of his fellow students, and the masters of his shinobi school executed him."

"But he faked his death?"

"Yes. His sensei underestimated his abilities, not knowing the extent of his kagenari. He faked his demise and escaped to Ryokō Owari with a few of his followers. Yet, he was not careful. To the Dragon's credit, Obo discovered Ezo mere weeks after his arrival."

"But he became delusional, afraid of the shadows that chased him."

"Wouldn't you? Ezo and his followers immediately removed him as a threat. However, Ezo did not kill Obo to win back his status as you say, to become the servant of a Great Clan again. Instead, he relished his complete autonomy, acting selfishly, whimsically, wildly as rōnin. He killed Obo and stole his identity in order to hide in plain sight. No one was looking for a gold-trade minister, and a Kitsuki investigator would be privy to secret information that could warn Ezo of danger. He thrived in the Fishers' Quarter amid the lower castes, far from eyes trained to detect illusions, a ruler among worms. No one knew of the infiltration until a few months ago, when somehow our spy network caught wind of a acting and infiltration school secretly operating here.

"As our scouts dug deeper, they found rumors of kagenari being used, stories among the peasants about magic brands and those who could step between shadows. That's when our informants discovered that Ezo had established his 'Shadow Den Dōjō,' where, as you say, he continued to experiment on his pupils, low- and high-caste alike, most of whom did not survive. We do not know how many he successfully granted his abilities, but we do know of his two youngest, the least discreet. Takao, who was branded with shadow. And Aoi, who somehow did not die during the ritual but whom the shadow brand could not stain.

"You see, Yojiro, his threat to the Scorpion was much more than the dispensing of young people. Ezo actually tampered with the powers of Heaven, degrading the Celestial Order and mocking the Three Oaths by establishing a rogue school—one without clan or purpose save his own. You see, Yojiro. He became ninja."

"Ninja," Yojiro repeated. The word felt bitter on his tongue, having changed so much in the last few days.

*Then Seno had truly been onto something. He must have somehow witnessed something that proved Ezo's arrival in his city ten years ago. "Truly capable, though unwise," as Obo had observed in his notes.*

"And this threatened our clan's very existence," Aramoro continued, jerking his hand from the water, as if bitten by a serpent. He clenched his fist. "Because of rumors of his success with Takao, several Scorpion shinobi leaders were willing to legitimize Ezo's Shadow Den Dōjō, adding it their ranks. However, that was before the Dragon Clan got ahold of the information. We learned that the Kitsuki had not only heard of Ezo and his execution but also suspected that he had faked his death. This meant Ezo was a liability. If we laid claim to such a character, turning a blind eye to his selfish corruption, our clan would risk being forever disgraced, perhaps even disbanded. And so, I was sent to eliminate him."

Yojiro frowned. "But why did you let yourself get caught? Surely, a more subtle elimination would have avoided political contention while not provoking the Kitsuki investigators."

"I wanted to provoke them!" Aramoro said, grinning. "Ezo and I had a long discussion about this when I spoke with him the day before his death. He did not agree with my decision in the end, and he tried to escape, but his death was swift. The least I could do for an old friend."

His own fight with Takao flashed inside Yojiro's head. He had barely survived, saved instead by luck and Aoi's interference. For Aramoro to have slain a shadow master in a dark street, without sustaining any injury, must have been an amazing feat.

"The involvement of a high-ranking Scorpion in the death of one of their investigators serves two functions," Aramoro continued. "The first is that our clan has sent a warning to the Dragon that not only do we know about their investigators' schemes here in Ryokō Owari but also that we do not allow them to act with impunity. Thanks to Ezo's convenient work over the last decade, we know they have no proof with which to come forward and accuse our clan of dishonorable acts. Threat of a public scandal dares them to reveal what they know, and if they take the bait, it will be the Kitsuki School of Investigation's downfall. Imagine them making the same mistake as that fool Seno! Calling the Storm Tigers ninja? Public disgrace is inevitable."

Yojiro bit his lip. "And what is the second function of your arrest? Is this where I come in? To punish me by forcing me to clean up after your public declaration of war on the Dragon Clan?"

"Ha! A task worthy of Kachiko's vengeance." Aramoro laughed, rubbing his hands together. "But no. Our goals were much less petty than that, Yojiro. I allowed myself to be arrested to send a public declaration to anyone, whether Dragon or Scorpion, that we, as a clan, will never tolerate ninja. We will hunt down and destroy all those who would defile Bushidō. We will punish those who would tamper with the Celestial Order and serve only themselves. And that, Yojiro, includes you."

Yojiro's stomach lurched.

"Me?"

"Yes, Yojiro. Your failure at the Tournament of the Emerald Champion was indeed unfortunate, but it also reeks of disobedience. Of selfish independence. Kachiko and several daimyō were worried that your behavior might lead you to betray our clan someday."

"I did not…" His voice crumbled before the memory of his vehement resolve at the Temple of Amaterasu. He had been ready to betray them. To exterminate them. To disband their clan. To be free of them forever. He was thinking as a rōnin, ready to burn down the world, as Denmaru had said. He could no longer call that honor. Only selfishness.

Yojiro sank down into his collar and crossed his arms. His heart, pricked through so many times by his clan in only a few weeks, felt raw. Fatigued. Yet…

*This was an exile of redemption. Ezo's life had been a parable Kachiko wanted me to see. Ezo walked the depraved road of the rōnin, a masterless samurai. Adrift on the waves, lacking the surety of a life in service to a Great Clan.*

*"Will you do the same, lapdog?"* Aramoro's twisted grin and sneering eyes seemed to say. *"Will you cling to your own whims, your own selfish desires? Will you destroy yourself, and force us to destroy you?"*

Yojiro steeled his face. He would not give Aramoro the satisfaction of seeing him bow.

"The next time I see you, Aramoro," Yojiro simply whispered, "you shall be a free man."

He turned and walked away, beckoning the guards to take Aramoro back to his cell. Motome ran up to him, her warm eyes bright with excitement.

"Did he tell you anything? Did he confess?"

Motome looked different. Smaller. More grey. Somehow, his eyes had changed. His body quaked under the solemnity of the moment. From the depths of his soul, through the muddled mists of confusion and worry, a pillar of clarity emerged.

He was a Scorpion, and without that, Bushidō was hollow.

He pulled his high collar a little higher around his neck, shielding more of his face.

"He did not confess," Yojiro said, heading toward the exit, away from Motome. "Aramoro is innocent. However, I know who killed Obo. Gather your dōshin and meet me at the Fortuitous Wind. Our murderer might still be there."

The lies burned his tongue as they left his mouth. He almost welcomed the sting.

# Chapter Eleven

Back in the Fishers' Quarter, Yojiro followed the gutter up to the Fortuitous Wind. The stench. The smoke. The shadows. None of it bothered him now. His purpose remained fixed. His promise to Toturi seemed small next to the impending disgrace of his entire clan. If the Scorpion could stand against ninja, to right their own wrongs and cleanse their ranks, they must be preserved to serve as Rokugan's underhand.

As Yojiro approached the inn, Denmaru and his squad strode by on their patrol Yojiro hailed the Thunder Guard captain and humbly bowed to him.

"Captain Denmaru," he began, his words stumbling over his newfound humility. "Forgive my ignorance. You and your soldiers put out that fire in the Licensed Quarter the other night, didn't you?"

"You were looking for any excuse to hate us. Your own clan. Just like that Otomo."

"You were right. I ignored the signs even when they happened right before my face, like with the Storm Tigers. Otomo-sama has been fabricating evidence of ninja for years now, hasn't he? Thanks to you, he failed last night, didn't he? So, he clumsily tried to implicate me."

"He burned down his own mansion seven years ago to do it, too." Denmaru grunted, folding his arms across his armored chest, the scars on his hands and face stretched tight in his resentment. "He claimed he saw a ninja there on the rooftop. He nearly set the entire Noble Quarter ablaze. So you see why Hyobu-sama and I stop him when we can."

*Obo must have seen one of Ezo's students. Perhaps the waterfalls were not so foolish.*

Yojiro's heart twitched, the weight of his upcoming task pressing down on all his bruises. He bowed and made a final farewell to Denmaru, and he entered the inn.

This time with no dishrag welcome.

Instead, Aoi, impersonating Jin once again, slumped over a straw broom, struggling with shaking hands to clear the last little grains of sand from between the floorboards.

Takao, again disguised as a fisherman, scrubbed the walls with hot water and ash, his brow furrowed in concentration.

Neither spoke to the other. The common room was empty, as if their silence had driven away their business.

"Jin-san, Ebi-san," Yojiro greeted them, wary of the dim corners of the room, his hand hovering ready to draw his weapon if necessary. "Good afternoon."

"What do you want?" Takao hissed, his hand lowering to his side, indicating the location of a hidden dagger.

Aoi grabbed Takao's arm, ignoring the threat. She propped her broom against the wall.

"Good afternoon, Magistrate," she said, bowing, attempting her best old servant imitation. "What can this humble servant do for you?"

"Much better, Aoi-san," Yojiro said, sorrow creeping into his heart, threatening to crush his resolve. He clenched his teeth. "Now, if you would be so kind as to reveal yourself."

"If you wish," she said, warily, sharing a skeptical glance with Takao before obliging. Her young face, wet eyes, and long hair appeared. She still wore the old man's clothes, but they fit her young woman's body, their appearance on Jin's frame having been part of the illusion. "What can we do for you, Yojiro-sama?"

Yojiro moved closer to them, lowering his voice to a whisper. "One of you needs to come with me."

"What for?" Takao snarled, ready to break free from Aoi if necessary.

"To be arrested for the murder of Kitsuki Obo, the man who sold street orphans to geisha houses throughout the city. This will keep the secret of Soshi Ezo, the man who branded youths with kagenari magic in his rogue shinobi school."

Takao and Aoi looked at each other, alarm stretched across their faces.

"Why us?" Takao demanded. "Aramoro is the one who killed Ezo-sama. And he got caught. He should take the blame."

"Aramoro-sama needs to go free," Aoi whispered, clutching tighter at Takao's arm, fear at the realization blanking her eyes as she stared into space. "For the clan."

"I can exonerate him," Yojiro explained. "I have enough evidence to use against either of you, but if one of you will confess, it will expedite things. You only have a moment to decide—"

"In here!" Motome shouted in the street. The three Scorpions turned to see the yoriki plunge into the inn with a dozen guards crowding in through the entrance.

Takao snatched Aoi's hand and bolted up the stairs, quick as lightning.

"Stop!" Motome yelled. She and her dōshin barreled past Yojiro in hot pursuit, their feet shaking the entire dilapidated building as they ascended after the young couple. Yojiro walked after them, knowing the two shinobi would use their abilities to escape, so speed was of no consequence. Takao had more than likely melted into shadow already, but Aoi only had one trick.

Motome and her dōshin spread out, pounding on all the doors and rushing into the rooms, the shouts and surprises of the tenants ringing in the air. The sound of crashing upstairs indicated she was tearing furniture away from walls and flinging belongings from closets, thorough in her search for two people who had apparently vanished. With many rooms in the inn, her search would surely last a few more minutes, despite the help of her guards.

Yojiro waited at the bottom stair. An old woman hobbled toward him, her back bent and her head bobbing in fear as she trembled down the steps to avoid the violent noise from above. Despite the posture, Yojiro could see the woman's movements were greatly exaggerated, not a steady, wary descent after decades of frailty. He put his hand on the woman's shoulder.

"You know, Aoi-san, you are a better choice than Takao for many reasons," he whispered into her ear.

"No. We shall not surrender," she said, her incongruous young woman's voice quivering in fear, lending an intense innocence to her wrinkled eyes. Motome's voice shook the ceiling as she ordered her guards to open all the windows and look down into the alleys, to climb onto the roof if necessary. Aoi swallowed. "We can escape."

Takao burst from the darkened crack of a backroom door, having doubled back for Aoi. He lunged at Yojiro, dagger in hand.

"Let her go!" he hissed, striking, but Yojiro had already learned Takao's attack patterns, and found them easier to navigate by the light of day. He dodged and then snatched Takao's arm where the shadow brand was hidden.

"This cannot be found on the body of a prisoner," Yojiro calmly stated, his heart breaking for them as he pleaded with Aoi. "This secret must be kept. Aoi-san, I know that somehow, the shadow brand did not stay on your skin. You healed without gaining its power."

Takao struggled in his grip, trying to shift the blade into the other hand. Yojiro twisted the wrist, and the knife fell to the floor.

"Aoi-san," Yojiro continued, keeping his voice low to avoid Motome's attention. "I know that Ezo still kept you, even when the shadow brand did not stick. He trained you in his impersonation craft instead. He gave you purpose. If you do this, you can keep Ezo's secret safe."

"Don't listen to him, Aoi," Takao interrupted, struggling in Yojiro's grip. "He is manipulating you. The Scorpion Clan murdered Ezo! And now they want to murder us, too!"

However, Aoi's old-woman face dissolved into her own, and her own shoulders hunched over in resignation. She turned to Takao, her dewy eyes wet with real tears. "I am sorry, but Yojiro-sama is right." She frowned, a world-weariness tainting her young face. "And without Ezo-sensei, we have no master. We must return to the Scorpion, rejoin the clan. Or else we have no purpose."

"We have purpose!" Takao insisted, his own hurt twisting his mouth into a bitter scowl. "You and I can carry on Ezo's school."

Aoi shook her head. "Ezo's school is nothing without a clan,

Takao. I've long thought this. We must do our duty to the Scorpion. I may be expendable to them, but through this, I find meaning." She turned to Yojiro, putting her hand on his arm. "I will go with you, Yojiro-sama."

"No, Aoi," Takao whispered, wrenching free of Yojiro to grab her shoulders and shake her. "I will not allow you to sacrifice yourself for this."

Aoi smiled at her lover, a last, sweet smile commanding all her lingering courage. "Do you remember our first lesson from Ezo-sensei? About loyalty to him as our master? You and I still live by it. Your anger is an expression of loyalty toward our sensei, honoring his death and seeking revenge against those who wronged him.

"My sacrifice will be my loyalty toward Ezo-sensei's school, to hide you, his greatest success."

Takao's face softened long enough for her tears fall onto his hands in their final shared moment.

Within seconds, Motome crashed back down the stairs.

"Yojiro-sama, you caught the girl!" She panted, fumbling down the steps with her guards. She gestured for them to bind Aoi. "Where is the boy?"

"He was just a bystander," Yojiro said, twisting his fingers into painful knots in his pockets. Takao had completely vanished. "No need to look for him. We have the person we came for."

"Yojiro," Aoi called to him as they finishing binding her arms, an intense hope struggling over the despair choking her voice. "Do you believe in reincarnation?"

Yojiro stared at her, wondering, begging the Heavens for the first time in his life for the Celestial wheel she longed for to be real.

"For those who keep the Celestial Order with duty and devotion, another life is promised," he said, his face growing solemn, relaxing into his next words, as though he were about to lie. He was not sure of their veracity. But he would tell her anyway. "If the Heavens care for any of us, you will be reunited in a future life, Aoi-san."

With that, the guards took her away.

"What was that about?" Motome asked as they abandoned the inn. She still had her jitte clenched tightly in her fist, as if afraid of an assault from some unknown source.

Yojiro straightened his collar again on either side of his face, shielding himself from the world of shadows.

"Some lies we just need, Motome-san," he said, turning to look at the gutter. The trickle of brown sewer water glittered as it ran downhill to empty into the Bay of Drowned Honor. He could no longer smell the stench.

# Epilogue

*Y*ojiro leaned over at his worktable, a slab of cherrywood before him, glowing warm under the undisturbed sun through his open windows. He slid weary fingers over the grain. A dark ripple here. A pale river there. The solitude of his craft calmed him. The strain of his mission to Ryokō Owari still trembled in his tired heart. The betrayal. The tragedy. The darkness. He had traded his own soul for a life. But he had also given up Aoi's life for their clan.

Soshi Aoi had confessed to killing Kitsuki Obo in revenge for his part in her sale to a geisha house as a child, only one victim of many. Her verbal confession was enough to convict her, and she would be executed within the week. Shosuro Takao had disappeared, taking the instruments of the Shadow Den Dōjō's rituals with him, leaving no hints of his next move. Yojiro hoped he would not see the shadow-branded shinobi again, but he was sure that revenge would drive them together again one day. Aramoro was released without penalty for his lack of involvement in the murder, though he stayed on in Ryokō Owari to enjoy the luxuries of the Licensed Quarter as a free man. Kitsuki Obo's ashes and belongings were on their way back to the Dragon Clan, although Yojiro knew the shipping caravan would be attacked by brigands, ensuring that everything, including Obo's ring, clothes, and desk, would be lost. Seppun Motome was praised by no one for her involvement in the case, many of her clues having been largely unneeded in convicting Aoi, and Otomo Seno had no interest in such minor murder cases anyway. Instead, had written his long letter to the Emerald Champion, reporting on his many exploits in purging his city of ninja, though he was still awaiting a reply.

Yojiro sighed. Motome had written a long parting letter to him, which he still kept in his breast pocket, next to the new ochre silk coin purse she had sent.

"I must admit that my bias against the Scorpion hindered my evaluation of Obo's sinister activities, an advantage he pressed for a decade. While I am still far from trusting the Scorpion in my city, I now know that there is more than Scorpion crime to look out for. I will attempt to work more closely with Captain Denmaru rather than against him, as you advised. In turn, I hope that you can continue to use your influence, and your sense of duty and honor, to move other Scorpion, especially those in the capital, to mete out true justice."

The irony of her words slapped him in the face. He had betrayed her most of all. However, there had been no choice. Their relationship of trust had been sacrificed on the altar of necessity along with Aoi. To loyalty. To the Scorpion.

*"When you visit again, I will fulfill my promise to take you to the Temple of Daikoku,"* she ended, forcing Yojiro to smile in spite of himself. *"Your friend, Motome."*

Yojiro pressed his sharp wood knife to the pulpy surface of the cherry block before him. A single wood shaving bloomed before his blade like the petal of a new flower.

*I should propose some policy changes to Champion Toturi about Ryokō Owari, to do her a favor. Perhaps starting with a promotion.*

A heavy rap at the door drew his attention.

"Enter," he called, setting his tool down in deference to his visitor.

The shōji screen slid open to reveal a tall, shadowy figure. Yojiro flinched instinctively, his hand already at his katana. He crouched in a defensive stance and prepared for the worst. However, no shinobi or brigand emerged from the dark. Instead, the open door revealed a grotesque visage of a crimson oni, fully fanged and horned. Its form was dressed in opulent red-and-black silks, the minute patterns woven into the brocade flickering like a rippling tide of fresh blood in the sun. Through the shining pits where the oni's eyes should be glimmered an unfathomable cunning. The man in the mask was the Scorpion Clan Champion, Bayushi Shoju.

Yojiro bowed low, lower than he ever bowed, as Shoju entered, mild tremors of fear and awe spreading throughout his chest. Though he had met the Clan Champion many times, he had never had a personal audience, let alone a personal visitation.

"Shoju-ue. You bless my workshop with your presence. Please, forgive the disorder."

Shoju waved away the flattery with a black-lacquered fan, uncharmed by the formality. The oni mask completely concealed his facial emotions, exaggerating every slight move of the body into a crucial language, mesmerizing to behold.

"You returned triumphant," Shoju boomed, his deep voice echoing from the depths of his oni mask, likewise devoid of telling tones or strains, his motives and intentions fully veiled. "My brother is free, and our clan is above reproach. Kitsuki Obo's scandalous activities in Ryokō Owari Toshi have swung the pendulum of power back to the Scorpion. The Dragon have been weakened, particularly our enemies among the Kitsuki investigators. You have done well."

"I humbly thank you for your praise, Shoju-ue," Yojiro said, bowing again.

"I was even impressed with your actions during the Tournament of the Emerald Champion, Yojiro-san," Shoju continued, taking up one of Yojiro's carving knives from the worktable and deftly spinning it in his fingers. "By giving Toturi that riddled hint, ensuring his win against Aramoro, you proved you could choose our clan interests over even Lady Kachiko."

Yojiro swallowed.

*Lord Shoju knows the whole truth...And yet, he is the only Scorpion who sees the tournament in this way. Not as a failure but as a benefit. Why?*

"You might have suspected that you were chosen for this mission in Ryokō Owari as some form of test," Shoju continued, absently inspecting Yojiro's wood block. "My wife believes she was

testing you, trying your limits of sacrifice…of self-debasement…
of pain." He plunged the knife silently into the wood where it stood
quivering, a trembling spire in the new slab. "However, I wanted
to see your limits too, Yojiro-san. I wanted to measure your loyalty
to the Scorpion, even in the face of our most precious secrets. The
dishonorable existence of shinobi proved the perfect trial.

"You are obviously ready for more crucial tasks. More powerful
influence. You are ready to take your place at my side and help me
save Rokugan."

"My lord," Yojiro stammered. He hoped his faltering sounded
like surprise instead of distress. The last fleeting hope of a life like
Motome's—simple, honest, honorable—seemed to fade forever
with those words. "I thank you."

"We shall speak again," the Scorpion Clan Champion replied.

Shoju departed as suddenly as he had appeared, leaving the
doorway dark and empty. Yojiro slid the door shut and wrenched
his knife free from his cherry plank. The tip was undamaged, having been slid perfectly into an invisible weak spot in the grain.

Yojiro wiped the sweat from his palms and calmed his breath.
*Will working with Shoju will mean more autonomy, more choice?*

Again, he attempted to carve into his cherry block, this time
starting from the hole that Shoju had left. The wood curls came
away easily, but all he could manage to do was widen the pit,
deepen the hole. He scoffed at himself and threw the tool down.

*No, working with Shoju will only mean more sacrifices.*
*More lies.*

He stared at the uncarved wood. He would begin again tomor-
row. The surface would wait, a form still full of a thousand possible
truths. As craftsman, he could shape it however he wanted. When
the time was right.

# About the Author

Mari Murdock is a freelance writer and literature/writing instructor who has worked with various game companies since 2014, including Alderac Entertainment Group, Gallant Knight Games, and Fantasy Flight Games. Having lived in Japan, Taiwan, and Hawaii, Mari loves world cultures, history, philosophy, and art and strives to incorporate what she has learned in her travels in her work. She is currently finishing up a Masters degree in oceanic post-secular modernism, and when she's not doing homework, you can find her GMing RPGs, cooking Japanese food, and going on adventures with her husband, Scott. Check out her blog at empusaegirl.tumblr.com and her curriculum vitae at marimurdock.weebly.com.

# Rokugan

## An Empire in Turmoil

A land where honor is stronger than steel. Here, the samurai of the seven Great Clans serve the Emperor as warriors, courtiers, priests, and monks. They live—and die—by the tenets of Bushidō.

The Scorpion Clan enjoys great favor with the Emperor as his confidants and advisors, but those at the top are doomed to one day fall. In the City of Lies, the very reputation of the clan is at stake, and the loyalty of its sworn samurai will be put to the test.

# SHOSURO AND SOSHI:
# THE BODY AND ITS SHADOW

Once upon a time, at the dawn of Rokugan, Lord Bayushi wandered the land in search of followers who could help protect Rokugan from threats unseen. His brother, Emperor Hantei, needed him to do the villainous, contemptible work the Empire would need, and Bayushi had no choice but to obey. As he traveled through the hills and forests, he stopped at an inn for the night. There, a stable boy with dull eyes and a head shaved for mites begged for a coin. However, Bayushi ignored him, eager for sleep, so the boy went away, his hunger flowing into despair.

The next day, while roaming the abundant fields of western Rokugan, Bayushi crossed paths with a sun-wrinkled peasant woman. She carried a basket of radishes, pale as the morning sky, and she offered them to him, shouting between her missing teeth, "A coin for the whole lot!" But the Kami ignored her and continued down the road, so the crone went away, curses upon her lowered voiced.

On the third day, the Kami drifted into a pleasure house, hoping to find a worthy follower there. All he found was a geisha with demure yet twinkling eyes who plucked a trembling melody on the koto for him. Frustrated, he turned to leave, only to be halted by the prick of steel against his throat.

"My Lord Bayushi will surely not leave a third time without giving me a coin," the geisha whispered into his ear, pulling her knife tighter to his skin.

The Kami smiled and gave this new acquaintance what she desired, knowing he had found a worthy follower. She would be the first member of the Scorpion Clan.

The stable boy, the peasant, and the geisha had all been Shosuro, an actress whose uncanny talent to mimic man, woman, child, or elder knew no bound. In truth, no one knew her real form, but the appearance of a woman seemed to be her favored act. She could become anyone she chose through mere skill of her craft floating through a thousand lives and more. However, when Bayushi discovered her, wandering alongside him through the provinces of Rokugan, Shosuro had been drifting rootless, squandering her talent with no real stage upon which to perform.

Enamored with the young mortal, Bayushi invited her into his arms and asked, "Would you, my artist with the many faces, be my eyes and my ears, wearing many masks and speaking false voices for the Empire's sake? Its enemies plot in their courts and on their battlefields, but you can mingle among them, as invisible as a trap beneath their feet, weaving a net to catch them in."

Shosuro, intrigued by this new part to play, agreed, adopting the Kami as her master and lover. Tasked with this clandestine defense of Rokugan, she founded the Shosuro family, a people dedicated to the art of disguise, intrigue, and stratagem, spies and infiltrators poised to discover all secrets of the land.

Shosuro adopted many faces and voices for the Scorpion Clan. A cringing servant in the house of a great lord. A daydreaming monk in a sleepy monastery. A covetous magistrate with a plump wife and fat children. She played some of these roles for years at a time, each one demanding she remake herself, weaving a new snare for her enemies. Eventually, in her passion for perfection, mere physical imitations began to bore her. Any child could play a serving girl, a monk, a magistrate, and her gift had unlocked the identity of any warrior, leper, or even Kami to her. She wondered if she had reached the limit of her skill.

One moonlit night, arising from Bayushi's bed, Shosuro gazed upon the shadows on the floor, and a silent voice called to her. She lit a candle but saw no one. Instead, these shades answered her, shifting, leaping, dancing with every whim of the flame. Their shapes grew and faded beneath the moon and her light with ease, and the depths of her heart longed for such boundless form, an emptiness so full, the power to change herself so entirely.

In those moments, Shosuro felt the pull of the Void, the element between all other elements, the negative spaces of reality. Branching far beyond the simple art of acting, she communed with this power, learning its shapes and abysses, mimicking the ways it manipulated the room around her. Soon, it revealed a new role for her—to play the part of shadow, to shape worlds from its fabric. Slowly, over years, Shosuro learned its language, forsaking her old path for that of a *shugenja*. Despite patient mastery of her new skill, this power was full of hungry prayers. It demanded more of her time, her talents, her traits, her very body in order to be wielded. The more she gave, the more it wanted. Frightened by its greed, she fled from its call, wringing her hands, tearing her hair, clinging to her lover Bayushi, afraid of losing herself.

The Heavens spun the Karmic Wheel, and years later, the Empire bled as the malevolent powers of Jigoku, the Realm of Evil, threatened to swallow Ningen-dō, the Realm of Mortals. Jigoku's champion, the fallen Kami Fu Leng, battled to cover the entire world in darkness, foul sorcery and armies of corruption at his command. On the terrible Day of Thunder, seven mortals rose to challenge him. Shosuro stood among them.

Led by Shinsei, these Seven Thunders fought Fu Leng in the Shadowlands, each falling, one by one, against his overwhelming power. In their death throes, Shiba stayed the churning hordes of oni and the undead while Isawa sealed their eternal enemy into the Black Scrolls. Both sacrificed themselves so that Shosuro could escape the Shadowlands with the scrolls. But it was not enough. Fatally wounded, her strength all but spent, Shosuro clutched her dangerous cargo, the armies of the Shadowlands not far behind. Despair gripped her soul, the bitterness of failure and a thousand years of darkness mere moments away.

So the shadow within her whispered. Its demand hung heavy in the air, pulsing between the elements in the Void. She could survive to complete her task—and see her beloved Bayushi again—if she surrendered herself to it. In an ultimate act of abandon, she accepted the shadow's bargain and relinquished her body and form—her pleasures, her memory, her spirit—to be remade in the darkness's image.

From this abandoned self emerged Soshi, a man with shadow branded upon his skin, his very soul, looking upon the world with new eyes, incarnated with new purpose. By becoming one with shadow, he was unbound by the constraints of mortal form. He could bend and flatten and travel with the dark—he could manipulate light and darkness to fashion intricate illusions, tricking the light in humans' eyes, making them believe the impossible. Manipulating the Void, he could transform reality.

So Soshi wandered Scorpion lands, testing his newfound skills. On the first day, he wandered to the base of the Seikitsu Mountains and stared up at their vast slopes. Communing with their shadows, he crept into a crag of their tiniest stone and stretched himself as vast as their highest peak. On the second day, he sped through rich fields, flickering between each stalk of rice as their shadows swayed and crossed.

On the third day, he caught a glimpse of Bayushi wandering along the road in mourning. Soshi approached his old lover, this time not in the form of an old peasant or beautiful geisha but as a mere silhouette, hiding within the gnarled shadow of an enormous muku tree. As Bayushi passed, believing himself to be alone, Soshi summoned his newfound power to craft an illusory rain. Surprised at the sudden shower of heavy drops from clouds that had not been there moments ago, the Kami paused, feeling the accompanying chill in the air, smelling the dampness of the earth rise. The illusion drove Bayushi to the shelter of the muku tree, and once again, the Kami felt the longed-for prick of steel at his throat.

"Does my Lord Bayushi fear the sunlight?" Soshi asked, embracing his old lover as he released the illusion, pulling the knife tighter against Bayushi's skin.

Bayushi gazed upon Soshi as the shugenja pulsed with the power of the shadow brand, ever-changing and ethereal, dancing between the elements to create shapes that had no body, illusions with no true form, and the Kami knew he had acquired another follower. He gripped Soshi by the arm and drew him close, his voice low and tender, "You are now my servant with no faces. You will fathom the depths of the Void, opening its doors for our clan to pass through, and you will make our enemies see what does not exist, sink into what has no depth, caught in a net of their own making. And you shall stay by my side."

Soshi agreed, this new Scorpion path unfolding before him. Tasked with the study of the secrets of reality, he founded the Soshi family, shugenja dedicated to the power of shadow, sacrificing all to discover and fashion the new shape of Rokugan.

# SHINOBI AND NINJA

Many in Rokugan are familiar with the term "ninja," though few can say it with an air of solemnity. Everyone knows that no such beings exist, and crude fables of these skulking assassins circulate among all circles of culture. For example, the peasants on the lands surrounding Otosan Uchi often whisper of the crimes of a ninja named Wokō, a rogue cast out from one of the Great Clans. Haunting the capital city's alleys at night and sneaking past Imperial guards, he murdered unsuspecting merchants for their fat purses and evaded capture by using forbidden magic. These and other tales of ninja never fail to depict ignominious villains who desecrate the tenets of Bushidō and to explain the fantastical nature of these criminals. A few tellers of these tales even recall rumors of an official Imperial ban centuries ago that forbade the use of such retainers and their shameful tactics—stories riddled with gossip about Bayushi shugenja and dark powers—but much of that talk has since faded into the vague, mundane reality of public knowledge.

Beyond the crass talk of the lower castes in unruly taverns hides the truth about these tales, which is that few clans are truly above the need for sly means should circumstances require it. Theft, infiltration, sabotage, and assassination sink far below the tenets of Bushidō, yet occasionally, honor may be a brittle dais upon which to gain victory. Sometimes, a servant must stoop to dishonorable tasks to achieve their masters' designs, sacrificing themself to keep their daimyō and clan pure. These samurai who would forfeit their own personal honor, fulfilling these most dishonorable duties for the good of the clan, are called *shinobi*: those who use stealth, those who endure.

In their role as the underhand of the Empire, the Scorpion retain the greatest number of shinobi, but other clans have members willing to make this sacrifice. Shinobi are motivated only by clan need, acting merely as weapons in the hands of their masters. Should they degrade themselves further to act for money or personal gain, they would become no better than the detestable Wokō, rōnin without purpose, which makes the term "ninja" a grave insult to the shinobi profession.

Due to the dishonor and exclusive secrecy surrounding their activities, shinobi exist as nonpersons, or members of the hinin caste, the lowest in society's Celestial Order, retaining no practical or even legal status. This means shinobi often abandon their real public lives to adopt new identities from all statuses and clans in order to infiltrate and manipulate as necessary. Although to kill a shinobi has no legal consequences, the discovery of one surely leads to gossip and scandals as people wonder about the shinobi's clan of origin. A shinobi's caste allows their clan to disavow responsibility should they get caught, making the shinobi truly a lone servant with no allies.

# Recruitment and Training

Young samurai and the occasional peasant who show particular proclivity and skill in agility, precision, stealth, or mercilessness may be handpicked to become shinobi. Before being extended an invitation to join a shinobi school, they must first pass secret tests administered by shinobi sensei who measure their capacity and willingness to adhere to the Three Oaths. For example, shinobi sensei may observe a potential student's propensity for discretion when privy to social secrets or their willingness to relinquish personal claims for the good of the clan. If they pass these trials, then the sensei approaches them with the proposition to join a dōjō.

Of the students who accept and abandon their former lives—the price of dishonor and existence as a nonperson—many adopt one or more less-conspicuous identities in the public eye, though some may retain their real identity only for the sake of appearances. Still other shinobi may destroy their public persona entirely to allow them to disappear discreetly from society. This may take the form of the clan fabricating their imprisonment or exile, or having the new shinobi fake their own death through an accident or illness. These measures allow the shinobi to fulfill their missions while avoiding the watchful eyes of enemies, especially enemy shinobi, who might find cause for suspicion.

When a shinobi successfully living out the Three Oaths' tenet of Patience reaches retirement age, meaning they have become incapable of physically or mentally performing their duties, the remaining tenets of Sacrifice and Secrecy also demand completion. This means that the shinobi must be slain to preserve their secret knowledge. This is often done by the shinobi's students or disciples. Ideally, if the old shinobi successfully passed on their knowledge to the next generation, then the contest ends in the students' favor. However, very rarely, the old shinobi may win, and worse yet, decide they are not yet ready for retirement.

In one infamous case, a sensei of the Scorpion's Tail School became corrupted. Though the causes were never determined, her clan leaders determined her unfit to continue as a shinobi. However, when her students went to dispatch her, she killed every single person in the dōjō and escaped to eradicate nearly all of the school's remaining practitioners. The Scorpion's Tail techniques were lost for several centuries.

## Double-Edged Blades

Ninjutsu training includes not only the techniques needed for infiltration, reconnaissance, and assassination, but also how to detect and defend against enemy shinobi. This includes securing buildings and camps, as well as ferreting out possible scouts and spies among a lord's own people.

# SHINOBI SCHOOLS

Because all shinobi schools are secret, some of the most elite dōjō are not even known among other shinobi of the same clan. The clans maintain a shroud of mystery over how many actually exist. Each shinobi school operates only according to its respective clan's requirements, taking orders from its clan champion, or sometimes those delegated authority from a previous clan champion to give the future leaders of the clan plausible deniability. In some cases, a new clan champion might even disband a dōjō when they feel it has outlived its usefulness, although some schools continue in secret, waiting to be called upon again to serve. The shinobi schools' emphasis on meeting clan need directs their various curricula; students training as shinobi only learn ninjutsu to the degree of proficiency needed by their clan. Rarely, a clan might assign a shugenja to become a shinobi, creating a formidable weapon.

Shinobi dōjō are scattered throughout Rokugan. Some exist in remote, hidden locations, while others operate in plain sight under false pretexts. The most prominent Scorpion shinobi dōjō is the Shosuro Butei Academy, located near Shosuro Palace. It operates publicly as a prestigious fumemboku acting school, and it secretly trains its shinobi students to specialize in impersonation for the purposes of infiltration. Other schools include the Thunder's Dagger Dōjō, which instructs Shosuro martial artists; the Brother's Gift Dōjō for Shosuro assassins and infiltrators; the Acting Academy for Shosuro impersonators; and the Hidden Moon Dōjō, where Soshi kagenari users and those branded by them are trained.

# THE THREE OATHS

Because shinobi disobey the tenets of Bushidō for the sake of their masters, they must live by their own ethics, a code called the Three Oaths. Though the need for Honor does not govern them, these ethics are a sacred duty of the shinobi just as Honor is for the samurai. To break any of the Three Oaths would signify the deepest betrayal of clan trust and a denial of the Celestial Order, resulting in instant termination. Each shinobi school of the different clans derives these three tenets from various sources; the Scorpion shinobi dōjō draw them from Shosuro's writings about her craft, as recorded in secret shinobi texts.

## SECRECY

*"The lips of a mask do not move. An actor's lines are as characters carved in stone."*
*– Shosuro*, A Chronicle of One Hundred Million Sacrifices

Secrecy defines the shinobi way of life. Involved in a world of covert missions, infiltrations, and concealed motives, where protecting the anonymity of masters and associates requires the utmost confidentiality on every level, shinobi must maintain this rule above all. A shinobi who has not mastered the art of Secrecy cannot accomplish their missions.

## SACRIFICE

*"Ten thousand deaths mean nothing to the actor, whose reincarnation wheel spins daily."*
*– Shosuro*, A Chronicle of One Hundred Million Sacrifices

Shinobi own nothing, yet must be prepared to give up more. They surrender their families and friends, possessions, titles, personal identities, emotions, and even autonomy. They are expected to sacrifice everything and anything to fulfill their purposes. These choices come without the glory, veneration, or even acknowledgement extended to other servants of the clans, making them more terrible than the sacrifices of other samurai and even more selfless.

## PATIENCE

*"Neither Sun nor Moon dictate my move. Only the part can do that."*
*– The Book of Silence*

Patience always has purpose. This oath refers not merely to timing and opportunity but also self-governance of impulses and reactions. A patient shinobi is never provoked, even by pain or death, because Patience indicates a perfect mastery over self and situations, even when the shinobi is faced with the unexpected.

# DISGRACE AND DISHONOR

Once a student joins a shinobi school, they begin formally learning ninjutsu in addition to completing their basic training as warriors or courtiers. Unlike other samurai, upon completion of their training, shinobi do not have a gempuku ceremony. Having relinquished all ties to their public life, they can invest little meaning in such ceremonies. However, this is when students may be appointed a new identity as part of a clan assignment. Those schools that focus on impersonation, such as the Shosuro Acting School, may have students craft a new persona for themselves as a test, and often, the creation of that first role is considered just as sacred a ritual as a gempuku.

There are hundreds of varieties of ninjutsu, and they fall into two categories: *fumemboku* (disgraceful) and *fumeiyo* (dishonorable). Ninjutsu considered fumemboku are the inherently neutral acts that can be dishonorably implemented and thus discredited, depending upon the situation. For example, skills such as acting, gathering information, and stealth can be learned and practiced by anyone in honorable situations. However, if they are used dishonorably, then their users are disgraced. Fumeiyo are exclusively dishonorable arts and usually are only performed by shinobi. These include acts such as sabotage, poisoning, and assassination, which cannot be done honorably, no matter the circumstance. This category also includes the specialized martial arts that use shinobi weapons, like the *shuko*, *shuriken*, *senbon*, and *fukiya*. Shinobi generally use these weapons from concealed locations against enemies at a distance, not in situations of honorable hand-to-hand combat, making them solely dishonorable means of attack.

The categorization of fumemboku and fumeiyo exists to help Great Clans evaluate whether they could use the services of a warrior or if they have special need for a shinobi. Under the Three Oaths, a shinobi simply does whatever they are commanded without complaint. Thus, their actions are judged not according to Bushidō parameters of what is honorable and dishonorable, but rather with respect to whether their results are ideal or flawed. For example, the fumeiyo act of poisoning is never honorable by Bushidō standards, which is why it is done by shinobi. However, if a shinobi were to get caught and poison themself to uphold the Three Oaths' tenet of Secrecy while embodying Sacrifice and Patience, this could be considered an ultimate shinobi accomplishment ideal for that situation. The highest ideal of a shinobi is to uphold all three principles in every situation.

# POISONCRAFT

One of the most dishonorable ninjutsu techniques is the art of poisoning. Shinobi learning to master the art of poisons begin with the Philosophy of the Five Venoms, the theories and foundational practices observed from poison in animals. The sources of the Five Venoms are the snake, spider, centipede, scorpion, and wasp. Poisoners are taught to retrieve and distill the poison from these animals for various uses, a nuanced and perilous art in and of itself. Shinobi also are encouraged to look to those animals as exemplars of their craft; they learn to emulate characteristics such as concealment, accuracy, and speed. In ancient times, poison alchemists placed one of each of the animals of the Five Venoms into an iron pot to fight. They believed that the venoms' potency would compound as the animals killed each other, with the last one alive embodying the culmination of all their power. Many other animals throughout Rokugan are also used for their mild to fatal toxins, such as jellyfish, puffer fish, snails, toads, lizards, bees, ants, and butterflies.

Beyond the animal sources, some plant-based poisons are among the most dangerous and versatile. The Shosuro Gardens boast several hundred varieties of toxic flowers, shrubs, trees, other plants, and mushrooms grown specifically for use by the Shosuro Poisoners Academy. Shinobi schools rarely craft antidotes to their thousands of concoctions. However, many Scorpion families retain shugenja specifically trained in the art of drawing poison from the body, just in case. Still, such measures are often futile, for the most potent of poisons spread so quickly that a shugenja cannot be summoned to attend to the victim in time.

# Giving Form to Shadow

Kagenari no Koto, "the art of shadow's form," calls upon the power of darkness that lay within Soshi and was adopted by him. Although its traditions have been passed down through the Soshi family over the centuries, the art is shrouded in secrecy. Even among the unconventional and furtive Scorpion Clan, its use is borderline forbidden due to its little-known and dangerous power, and it is only utilized under the gravest of circumstances. Instead, most Soshi shugenja rely upon the more traditional method of communing with the Fortunes to ask for their blessings. Only the highest-ranking daimyō of the Scorpion families are aware of kagenari's existence and the location of the dōjō where it is taught, and even then such knowledge is imparted on a strictly need-to-know basis.

The ways of kagenari are taught only to the most promising members of the Soshi—those who are chosen by the Soshi family daimyō. The selection process is mysterious, but many of those chosen are said to have an innate connection to the Void. Although some truly gifted students go on to be trained in the way of shinobi as well, practitioners of kagenari may instead imbue a non-kagenari practitioner with the shadow's blessing through a brand, a marking which imprints the powerful properties of shadow directly onto the skin.

Kagenari and its associated shadow brands give its wielders the ability to control and literally become one with shadows, allowing them to alter the constraints of their physical form, such as shape, size, and movement, to match the surrounding darkness. When cloaked in the shadows, the branded can see the unseen and cast their senses to places far beyond their physical limitations. They can detect the nothingness in others and manipulate its power to daze or disorient their targets. Only the Ishiken—the Void shugenja of the Phoenix Clan—are capable of similar feats.

The process of being shadow branded is long and excruciating, with varied, sometimes unforeseen and unprecedented, results. The rituals must be undertaken during the dead of night under a new moon, when darkness reigns, with the light of but a single candle to guide the practitioner's hand. The kagenari masters and their students gather in the deepest of caves, subterranean vaults, or abyssal tombs, or in the legendary Hidden Moon Dōjō itself, the stronghold of the Soshi. The rituals of the Hidden Moon Dōjō are said to be especially lavish and excruciating, all the better to heighten the potency of their brands. Many rituals may accidentally terminate in death, while some effects may not manifest until months or years after the branding. Many of those who survive the ritual have no memory of the event, and often, there is no body remaining when the branding ritual goes wrong.

To the trained eye, the brand appears as an intricate black labyrinth of swirls and knots on the skin, resembling a tattoo. There is speculation as to whether changes in pattern affect the bearer. The mark can be administered to different parts of the body, but those marked rarely get more than one brand due to the extreme risk. Although the brand can be seen clearly in dim light, some observers have noticed that it may completely disappear in the light of the sun. There have also been accounts of shadow brand bearers who can no longer endure the light of day, having dedicated themselves wholly to the darkness. Still other reports claim that eventually, branded persons may disappear altogether, swallowed by their own shadows. The fact that elderly shinobi bearing shadow brands are exceptionally rare seems to suggest that this is so.

## KAGE-DŌ

*"In the beginning, before the universe was created, there was only Nothing. In its perfection, it was alone, but whole. Through fear, desire, and regret, the Nothing was fragmented into ten thousand shards of reality, which coalesced into the jealous gods and the warring elements.*

*"To seek the Realm of Shadow is to return to the beginning. There, pain and suffering is no more, for nothing exists to distract from the Truth.*

*"It is the fate of the universe to return to the beginning. All that was done shall be undone."*

– *Soshi*, The Way of Shadow

# SECRET SHINOBI TEXTS

Master shinobi lead and teach at the shinobi schools. Over the centuries, the styles, practices, and teachings of those sensei have been gathered into secret shinobi texts. Many of these are recorded using code, some remaining secret and off-limits even to shinobi students. Though dozens of publications exist, three of those implemented by the major dōjō are the most famous.

*A Chronicle of One Hundred Million Sacrifices:* This volume, compiled by Sensei Chiyome, is the most used primer for all training of shinobi. It contains the basic knowledge, practices, and principles for the shinobi way of life. In it are numerous sections that shinobi must master before being allowed to accept missions. Besides instructions on emulating the Three Oaths, the volume includes definitions and degrees of espionage, overviews of defensive and offensive strategies, the basics for controlling and manipulating emotion and overcoming pain in its various forms, and details of the inevitable sacrifices that accompany these activities.

*The Book of Silence:* This text covers the art of silent killing, and though its origin is unknown, it has been largely adopted by some of the more elite assassination schools, such as those within the Brother's Gift Dōjō and the Thunder's Dagger Dōjō. Its pages include diagrams of the body marked with specific points for attack. One section outlines the crafting of specialized tools and weapons for the task, while another records strategies for overcoming obstacles such as water, walls, and guard animals while using environmental factors like weather or daylight for advantage. *The Book of Silence* emphasizes the doctrine of losing all markers of identity in order to blend with one's surroundings, insisting that novices begin training for these practices by taking a vow of silence.

*The Sea of Merging Rivers:* What is referred to as a single text is actually a vast collection of scrolls, each unique to its province, leaders, or shinobi. These scrolls record the history of clandestine shinobi activity over the centuries, with room for additions as they unfurl. Information regarding strategy, training, weapon use, leadership, and philosophy are recorded in these volumes. Some scrolls contain similar material, as schools may cross paths or trade students. Some also include passages taken from the lost writings of Shosuro and Soshi, affording their owners rare and formidable insight into shinobi power. These scrolls are scattered all over the secret shinobi libraries of Rokugan, and few master shinobi have read more than two or three. No one knows how far or deep this sea goes.